REUNITING WITH THE BILLIONAIRE

THE SUTTON BILLIONAIRES SERIES, BOOK 2

LORI RYAN

Copyright 2020, Lori Ryan.
All rights reserved.

This book contains material protected under International and Federal Copyright Laws and Treaties. Any unauthorized reprint or use of this material is prohibited. No part of this book may be reproduced or transmitted in any form or by any means, electronic or mechanical, including photocopying, recording, or by any information storage and retrieval system without express written permission from the author/publisher.

OTHER BOOKS BY LORI RYAN

The Sutton Billionaires Series:

The Billionaire Deal

Reuniting with the Billionaire

The Billionaire Op

The Billionaire's Rock Star

The Billionaire's Navy SEAL

Falling for the Billionaire's Daughter

The Sutton Capital Intrigue Series:

Cutthroat

Cut and Run

Cut to the Chase

The Sutton Capital on the Line Series:

Pure Vengeance

Latent Danger

The Triple Play Curse Novellas:

Game Changer

Game Maker

Game Clincher

The Heroes of Evers, TX Series:

Love and Protect

Promise and Protect

Honor and Protect (An Evers, TX Novella)

Serve and Protect

Desire and Protect

Cherish and Protect

Treasure and Protect

The Dark Falls, CO Series:

Dark Falls

Dark Burning

Dark Prison

Coming Soon – The Halo Security Series:

Dulce's Defender

Hannah's Hero

Shay's Shelter

Callie's Cover

Grace's Guardian

Sophie's Sentry

Sienna's Sentinal

For the most current list of Lori's books, visit her website: loriryanromance.com.

ACKNOWLEDGMENTS

Thank you to my wonderful husband for his patience and support. Thank you to Susan Smith for her endless brainstorming and reading and to Patricia Thomas whose editing proved invaluable. Thank you to Patricia Parent, my final set of eyes, for cleaning up after me.

I'd like to thank Dr. Kerry Weisz for her consultation on canine veterinary medicine and for her care of the real Rev. To read more about the dogs that are featured in the book, visit my website: loriryanromance.com.

I would also like to thank Jocelyn Stohl for her expertise in search and rescue operations. I apologize to search and rescue handlers everywhere for taking the liberty of having my characters do everything wrong (take matters into their own hands, leave the scene, you name it). It was necessary to the story! I am always in awe of the dedication and expertise that search and rescue handlers and their dogs have and hope someday to write a novel that will truly showcase the amazing work done by these professionals.

Thank you to all of the friends and friends-of-friends who read the pre-release version for me. I owe you all so much.

To read more of Lori's books, visit her at loriryanromance.com.

FOREWORD

If you love this book and want to read two novellas in the series for free, sign up for my newsletter here and I'll send them to you: loriryanromance.com/penalty-follow-up.

CHAPTER 1

*J*ill Walsh groaned as she watched the tan Jaguar pull up her driveway and park behind the moving van.
Crap.
She rolled her head backward, to the left, then the right. Slowly, slowly, trying to ease the tension from her body. It didn't work. Her teeth seemed welded together as her jaw refused to unhinge.
Are you kidding me?
Jill didn't bother to approach the car. If Jake insisted on coming today after she told him not to, he could damn well get out of the car and come to her.
Another groan escaped Jill's lips as Jake opened the car door and did just that.
"I told you not to come," Jill said not looking his way. She continued to watch the movers as they carried out the larger pieces of furniture. Most of the furniture would go into storage since her grandparents' home, which she would be living in temporarily, was already furnished. Only her photography equipment, her clothes and a few personal items were going to Westbrook with her.

"I thought I should be here. Just in case you need me," Jake answered with that pitying little smile on his face.

It irked the hell out of Jill that she still had feelings for her ex. That even though Jake treated her like a two-year-old, and even though he'd left her for his mistress after seven years of marriage, and even though he was an obnoxious jerk who just couldn't leave her alone, a part of her still wanted to rewind the clock and go back to the way things were before Jake told her he wanted a divorce.

Jill didn't answer him. It was a waste of breath. Clearly, if he listened to her, he wouldn't be here right now.

"Ma'am, you said there were things upstairs you're setting aside for Goodwill? Do you want to show us what to leave for them?" asked one of the movers.

"What? She's not giving anything away," said Jake. He stepped between Jill and the mover.

Jill gritted her teeth, her breath bursting out as she stepped around Jake.

"Yes, Jake. I am." Jill turned to address the moving man who now looked uneasily back and forth between Jill and Jake.

"All of the furniture in the master bedroom is going to charity. Can you move it downstairs, please? They're going to come take it after we finish up here," Jill said.

"What? Why are you giving the furniture away? It's perfectly good. I gave you the furniture so you wouldn't need to get anything. I'm trying to take care of you and you're giving it away?"

He loved to sound like the hero in the divorce settlement. A big man, taking care of poor little Jill.

She closed her eyes and began to count. *One...two...three... Oh to hell with it.*

"Yes, Jake. I'm giving away the damn furniture," Jill said, rounding on him as the movers retreated back into the house, away from the awkward tension of watching strangers argue. "Do you honestly think I want the bedroom furniture? That I would sleep in the bed where you slept with her?" Jill swallowed hard as she tried to finish the sentence that stuck in her throat.

Jake didn't look the least bit chagrined. "It's perfectly good furniture, Jill."

"You're unbelievable, Jake." For what felt like the tenth time since Jake arrived only a few short minutes before, Jill closed her eyes, took a deep breath and tried to center herself. Tried to let the feelings wash off her. Tried to release the tension.

"I'd like you to leave, Jake. I asked you not to come here and I'd like you to leave," Jill said, her eyes still closed.

"I just want to help you." He was indignant, as if Jill were being insensitive to *his* needs.

She opened her eyes and leveled a shuttered stare at him. "I need you to leave. I need a clean break, Jake. I need you to leave me alone and let me move on. You've clearly moved on with Missy." The name felt like acid coming out of Jill's mouth. "Let me move on."

She wrapped her arms around her body, hugging herself tight and turned back to watch the movers bring the last few boxes out of the house she'd shared with the man she'd loved with all her heart.

When the sale of the house had gone through yesterday, she had finally been rid of the last piece of communal property. She now needed to be rid of the memories and the heartache. Distance herself from her failed marriage. From the feelings she couldn't seem to get away from.

It was several more minutes before Jill felt him move away. She really didn't understand what he wanted. Why come around if he didn't want to be married to her anymore? Was it guilt? Control? Was he trying to keep her waiting in the wings in case he changed his mind?

She didn't understand his motives and didn't care at this point. In the beginning, his continual presence had given Jill hope. Now, she didn't want hope. She wanted this over. Over and done with for good.

A moment later, she heard his car start, listened to it as it pulled down the driveway. She began her neck rolls again. Slowly rolling back, left, right.

Breathe, Jill. Back, left, right.

Nope, didn't help a damn bit.

CHAPTER 2

*A*NDREW WESTON WALKED into the coffee shop in the lobby of the offices of Sutton Capital where he had been Chief Financial Officer for the past five years. He didn't look like your average corporate officer, dressed as he was in jeans and a polo shirt.

He grabbed a paper cup and lid from the stack on the counter and smiled at the two women next to him as he poured much-needed caffeine into his cup.

"Morning, Margie, Donna." Margie and Donna worked in the mailroom at Sutton. They were always together, like two halves of a whole. And they hit on Andrew any chance they got.

"Andrew, when are you gonna stop leading us on and just choose one of us? It's not fair to keep us waiting for a decision," Margie said with a flirty smile.

"Yeah, just pick one, Andrew. We've been fighting over you long enough. Put us out of our misery," Donna said.

Andrew laughed. The two of them knew as well as any woman that Andrew never dated anyone in the office. In fact, he didn't really date. He slept with women, but that was it.

But they teased him just the same. It had become a game.

"Sorry, ladies. How can I possibly choose between two such

gorgeous women? And, if I did choose, one of you would be heartbroken and I'd feel guilty. It might keep me up at night and then I'd lose my beauty sleep. Can't do it, ladies." Andrew laughed as he walked to the counter.

He smiled at the balding man behind the cash register. "Hi, Pete. Put Margie and Donna's coffee on my bill. And, I'll take a bagel, too, please," Andrew said. He put cash on the counter, grabbed his bagel and coffee and took off for the elevators.

When he stepped off on the twenty-sixth floor of the building, it took a split second to realize something wasn't right. His assistant, Debbie, rushed down the hall toward him with an anxious look on her face that put him instantly on high alert.

"Andrew," Debbie called out to him from a good ten feet away. "Lydia just called. Your grandmother fell on ice on her front walk. They're taking her to Yale-New Haven Hospital. They think she's broken her hip."

Lydia was the housekeeper and cook who had lived with his grandmother since Andrew could remember. She was as much a part of his family as his grandmother herself. Lydia was in her sixties now and his grandmother was rounding eighty this year.

Andrew turned back toward the elevator without waiting for Debbie to tell him what he already knew. She didn't need direction. Debbie anticipated Andrew's needs before he figured them out himself.

Andrew said she was responsible for at least seventy percent of his success. He knew Debbie would have already cancelled his appointments for the day. She also would have told Lydia that Andrew would be there as fast as he could.

He raised his hand to his ear. "I'll call you," he said as the elevator doors shut. Andrew stared at the numbers as the elevator counted down to the garage then ran back to his car with no other thought in his mind than he needed to get to his grandmother.

As soon as his car cleared the garage, he spoke.

"Dial Debbie."

The car's Bluetooth system answered in its stilted computer-generated voice, "Dialing Debbie."

"I'm here," said Debbie, picking up on the first ring.

"Let Jack know I'll be taking two weeks off," Andrew began.

"Already done," Debbie said. "I've got Paul and Katelyn taking over most of your meetings. I cancelled everything they couldn't cover."

Andrew's breath came out with a large whoosh as relief washed over him. He had the support he needed to care for his grandmother.

Nora Weston was not your typical grandmother. She was spunky and eccentric and didn't take crap from anyone, but she was also warm and caring and the most loving person in Andrew's life. She had always been there for him and he would always be there for her.

"Can you look into nursing care and rehab specialists that will come to the house? As soon as I know the extent of her injuries, I'll let you know the exact care she'll need, but for now, let's just see where we can get the best care. It needs to be in-home though. Nora wouldn't handle going to a rehab center or nursing home," Andrew said.

"Got it. I think Mary Shaver's mom needed nursing care recently. I'll see who she used," Debbie said.

"There's a carriage house on Nora's property. I'll move in there temporarily. Can you arrange to have some things from my condo packed and sent over? It's furnished so I just need clothes, toiletries, that kind of thing. My bike. Have them bring my bike over." Andrew liked to ride on the days he didn't go to the gym or play basketball with Chad and Jack, the cousins who were his two closest friends.

"Done."

Andrew paused.

"Still there, Boss?" Debbie asked when the pause grew.

"I should have taken better care of her." His chest tightened as he thought of Nora falling, of the pain and fright she must have felt. It hurt him to think about. "I should have realized Nora and Lydia were both getting older. Taking care of that house alone is too much for them. They need more permanent help than just a lawn guy and help with the cleaning occasionally."

"Nonsense," Debbie said, her tone sharp enough to cut off Andrew's pity party. "None of us ever knows when these things will happen. Nora hides any needs she has quite well and she wouldn't let you dote on her. You had the sidewalks shoveled and driveway plowed by a service. Nora wouldn't accept more than that. She would have scoffed at a full-time groundskeeper. We'll just set things up differently now that we know she needs more help. That's all we can do."

"Okay," Andrew said, but he still felt the guilt.

His parents didn't believe in hugs and kisses or giving encouragement. Growing up, no one other than Nora had told Andrew she was proud of him. She'd been the one to tell him to follow his dreams.

Andrew's parents were concerned only for their reputation and accumulating wealth. And when his parents didn't like the way things were going in Andrew's life, they paid people to change things.

The last payoff, almost eight years before, had resulted in Andrew cutting all ties to his mother and father. But he still had Nora. She had always been there for him as he grew up and he thought of her more as a parent than he did his true mother or father.

"I'll call you when I know something," Andrew said.

"I'll start arranging things from this end," Debbie said. He knew Debbie likely had half of the items on her list completed as they spoke.

As he navigated the quick ride through downtown New Haven

to the hospital, he thought of all his grandmother had done for him over the years. He had never really understood how she was so different. His mother was her daughter, but they were nothing alike.

When his parents didn't bother to stay in the States for Christmas or summer breaks, Nora sent for him.

She brought him home from boarding school to her estate in Westbrook so often Andrew thought of her estate as his home. She was the one who stood up to his parents when he wanted to go to sports camp instead of the academic camp his parents had lined up.

Nora went to his graduation from high school, then college, and finally Yale Business School. Andrew's parents did not.

She backed Andrew when he decided to go to Yale instead of working at his father's marketing firm. And when his mother and father had finally breached all reasonable boundaries, trying to control who he loved and married, Nora cut ties with Andrew's parents at the same time he did.

His parents wouldn't be at the hospital for Nora today. In fact, they wouldn't even be told Nora was injured.

It might seem cold to outsiders, but after what they'd done, there was no way he wanted them involved now.

Andrew pulled into the parking lot at Yale-New Haven Hospital and jogged across the covered walkway that connected the parking lot with the hospital building. He spotted Lydia at the front desk in the Emergency Room filling out paperwork.

"Lydia, where is she?"

Strain and worry lined Lydia's face.

"They took her upstairs to x-ray, sweetheart, but the doctor is already fairly sure she'll need surgery. If you sign here, I'll finish her paperwork, and you can go on up and be with her."

Andrew signed the paperwork, kissed Lydia on the cheek, then went to find the elevators to take him up to radiology. Lydia joined him twenty minutes later when he moved to the surgical waiting room. They settled in for a long wait while Nora's hip was pinned back together.

By the time he left the hospital four hours later, Debbie had already researched the type of surgery Nora was undergoing and the aftercare that would be needed. She would have to spend some time in the hospital but Debbie had arranged for more help at the house to be sure Nora and Lydia wouldn't want for anything.

For once in his life, the ridiculous amounts of money sitting in Andrew's bank accounts would be put to good use.

A week later, Andrew had Nora settled back home with around-the-clock nurses and a physical therapist scheduled every second day to help with rehabilitation.

The clean nature of the break in her hip and the fact that Andrew was able to provide twenty-four hour in-home care meant that Nora avoided a stay in a rehabilitation center. He wasn't sure she would have put up with one if the doctor had insisted. Nora might be loving and caring with him, but she could pitch a fit if things didn't go her way.

Andrew hired a full-time groundskeeper and maintenance man. And he hired a cleaning service to take over the house cleaning and another service to deliver groceries twice a week. Lydia drew the line at letting him bring in someone else to cook.

"No one's taking over my kitchen," she had said firmly and Andrew decided the fight probably wasn't worth having. Besides, he had a soft spot for Lydia's cooking. He wasn't sure he could give up the meals she stocked in his freezer on a regular basis.

He watched as Nora was settled into the hospital bed they'd had set up in a downstairs sitting room so she wouldn't have to go up and down the stairs.

"We can have a lift put on the stairs eventually."

Nora shot him a look he knew too well.

"You will not."

He grinned at her imperious tone. The fall hadn't slowed her spirit at all.

"This is a temporary health setback. You're not to make any permanent changes to my home." She actually sniffed and tossed her nose in the air. "Especially not one so ugly as that."

She frowned as Lydia walked in the room with a tray of food. "Andrew wants to hack up my staircase and add a lift."

Lydia stopped in her tracks and stared at him as though Nora had just told her he tried to chop her head off while Lydia was off getting her a sandwich.

"You want to do what?"

He only laughed and raised his hands in surrender. It was hopeless. He'd already had to fight to get Nora to accept his money for the new staff.

"I've got plenty of my own damn money. I can pay for things myself," she'd said.

Andrew knew that stubborn tone in her voice, but he also knew if Nora was the one to hire the extra staff, she'd eventually just let them all go when she thought she no longer needed them. If he hired the staff, he could decide how long they stayed.

Controlling? Yes.

But, Andrew wasn't taking any more chances on Nora's safety. Nora had capitulated only when Andrew told her he needed some way to alleviate his guilt. He laid it on thick, telling her she needed to let him do these things so he could live with himself after what he'd let happen to her.

"Oh, for heaven's sake," she finally said, literally throwing her hands up in the air. "If you must."

And they'd left it at that.

Now they'd all taken to eating dinner sitting on the couch in Nora's temporary bedroom to keep Nora company.

As Lydia brought in peach cobbler for dessert, Nora piped up with news that jolted Andrew back into his teen years.

"Jillie Walsh just moved back in next door, Andrew. Do you remember Jill?"

Nora knew damn well that Andrew remembered Jill. When he was fifteen, he had the biggest crush of his life on the next-door neighbor's granddaughter, Jill.

Andrew hadn't been very good at hiding his crush when Jill was eighteen and he'd only been fifteen. She came to visit her grandparents many times. But the summer that Andrew was fifteen, she spent two months with them before she went off to college. Andrew spent most of the summer at his upstairs window watching her swim in the Walsh's pool.

He didn't know if Jill knew but Nora had definitely caught on to the reason for his sudden attachment to the upstairs window. Luckily for Jill, her bedroom was on the other side of the house or Andrew would likely have watched a lot more than Jill in her bathing suit by the pool.

"Really? I didn't think the Walshes lived next door anymore," Andrew said.

Andrew's years in the corporate world had at least honed his skill at hiding his feelings so he was able to act a lot more casually about Jill this time around. But he wasn't feeling nonchalant on the inside, which was pretty ridiculous given how many years had passed.

The mention of Jill's name began a slow burn in Andrew's body. He thought back to her long blond hair and captivating hazel eyes. Andrew hadn't seen eyes like that on another woman in all these years. And no woman he had been with lived up to his fantasies about Jill. Not even Blair, the woman he'd once loved.

He wondered briefly if even Jill herself could live up to his fantasies, but he had a disturbing feeling an older, more mature Jill would live up to them and then some.

"They moved to South Carolina to live near their son two

years ago but they kept the house. It's been empty until now, but Jillie was divorced in September and she wanted to relocate. She's moved into their house while she figures out what she wants to do."

It didn't surprise Andrew that Nora already had the whole story behind Jill's reappearance. He was always amazed at how quickly Nora and Lydia had the scoop on everyone in the neighborhood.

"Wow," said Andrew, "I didn't even know she was married. Where has she been all these years?"

"She and her husband lived in Hartford. Mrs. Berlinger down the street spoke to her the other day but Jill didn't tell her much about the divorce. No kids, so it was a clean break," Nora said.

"Jill's a photographer. Nature pictures, I think." Lydia added that tidbit to the story as she cleared the peach cobbler dishes.

"Mrs. Berlinger said Jillie will be staying in her grandparents' house until she figures out where she wants to buy something of her own," Nora said. "You should go over and say hello tomorrow. I'm sure she'd be happy to see a friendly face now that she's back."

Andrew helped Nora back into her bed and raised the safety rails on the side. She scowled and he knew she would make Lydia lower them after he left.

"Maybe I'll run over in the morning."

Andrew tried to sound casual even as his body tensed at the thought of seeing Jill again. It was stupid, but he had thought of Jill on occasion over the years and sometimes, when he saw a blond woman in a crowd, he would even crane his neck to see if she was Jill.

None of them had been Jill, so the thought that she was once again just next door caused fantasies to race through his mind.

CHAPTER 3

*I*t was no surprise that an hour later Andrew found himself standing at the upstairs window of the carriage house. He looked out onto the Walsh's property, thinking about the girl next door.

He didn't actually expect to see her, but when he thought about what he was doing, he kicked himself for acting like an adolescent jerk. He was just about to turn away when a light spilled out onto the backyard.

The back door opened and a large brown dog ran out into the yard, barking and leaping in the snow. Jill followed, wrapped in a blanket. Andrew stepped back a few inches to avoid being seen, but he couldn't help watching when Jill looked up at the stars.

The grown up version of Jill Walsh was more sexy than ever. If she was even half as sweet and kind-hearted as he remembered, he couldn't imagine how her husband let her get away. Her ex must be a first-class idiot.

Andrew groaned as Jill tilted her head back and caught snowflakes on her tongue. Jealous of a snowflake. He'd sunk to new levels.

Shaking his head at himself, he walked into his bathroom, turned on the shower, stripped down, and doused himself with cold water. He had a feeling it wouldn't work, but he had to try to wash away the sight of snowflakes melting on Jill Walsh's tongue.

∼

Jill was content to be back in her grandparents' home. Since the morning ten months ago when Jake announced he loved someone else and wanted a divorce, she'd felt lost and anchorless.

But this home was filled with happy memories for her. Jill didn't have many friends in the area since she only visited her grandparents during the summers and hadn't been here in years, but she figured she'd get out and meet people. She'd make friends eventually and feel more settled.

Girlfriends. Only girlfriends. Jill didn't need any men in her life at this point. She'd been completely blindsided when Jake said he wasn't happy.

She had believed in their love, their marriage, and their commitment to one another. She thought they were happy. At this point, she couldn't imagine letting herself trust that way again. After all, even if she thought she was in love, how could she trust in another person's feelings, in the strength of their commitment to one another after the colossal mess of her marriage?

She couldn't. It was that simple. Jill couldn't trust like that ever again. What she was feeling right now hurt too much to risk going through with another man.

She frowned, knowing it would be sad to live without love in her life, but she just didn't see any way to let herself take that kind of chance.

Okay, so maybe she'd have to let up on the girlfriends-only thing. She'd just keep anything that did happen with a guy completely casual. Yeah. A good no-strings-attached fling every once in a while wouldn't hurt. But that would be it.

She opened the back door and stepped out into the yard, watching Rev, her chocolate Labradoodle race off to chase snowflakes. That dog was always happy, no matter what he was doing, and his uncontained pleasure with everything managed to bring a smile to Jill's face.

She looked up at the night sky. She was probably ready for a good fling to help erase the sting of her husband's betrayal. It was odd, really, the way she felt after the divorce.

Jill was still confident in so many ways. She knew she was smart, and for the most part, still felt attractive. She knew she was a good friend, had a good sense of humor and that she was a talented photographer. She knew and believed all those things.

But even knowing all that, there was still a nagging sense of... inadequacy. The feeling of being not enough somehow. Like she should have been able to keep her husband from straying.

Jill's parents had been together for fifty-two years and were still happily married. They'd built a strong and loving marriage that lasted. Why couldn't she? She asked herself a million times since that morning what was wrong with her that her marriage didn't last.

She even wondered if her inexperience in the bedroom before she married Jake had left her ill-equipped to please him and keep him satisfied. Her head told her that was foolish. Jake was the one at fault for his behavior.

In her head, she knew that. Her heart just had trouble believing it.

She sat down on the rocker on the back porch and watched the snow fall. Her mind surprisingly wandered to the boy who used to visit his grandmother next door. Where had Andrew Weston ended up? Though Andrew had been three years younger than her the last summer she'd spent here, his attention had been hard to miss.

It had been flattering, but his fifteen years to her eighteen stopped the adulation from going any further. Despite that, even then, Jill knew Andrew would grow up to be more than just good looking someday.

Jill felt a shiver of excitement rush through her as she tried to imagine a grown-up Andrew Weston paying that kind of attention to her. What had only been flattering in a cute, kid-next-door kind of way back then might be downright exciting now.

She would bet anything he'd filled out nicely. She could imagine broad shoulders and muscles on his once-skinny frame. A lot of muscles. He'd been a runner back then. Did he still run now?

With a shiver that had nothing to do with the cold, Jill called Rev, smiling as she watched her dog race back to her. She'd give anything to be as happy as that big, dumb dog.

They walked back in the house together where Jill headed off for a restless night's sleep. Her dreams that night were heated and racy, filled with a grown-up version of the boy next door, doing more than watching her as she lay by the swimming pool.

CHAPTER 4

*A*ndrew poured his coffee and walked over to the window to see how much snow had stuck to the ground the night before. He scratched his face as he went. He was sleeping in later while on leave from the office and had let the scruff on his chin grow.

The snow had just dusted the ground and was already melting away in the mid-morning sun. Andrew was treated to another sight that was more welcoming than snow.

Jill Walsh was back in her grandparents' backyard. He watched as she stretched up toward a tree limb. She hung what looked like a saltlick in a small metal frame mounted on the tree. Jill's dog ran in circles around her as she walked across the huge backyard toward another tree. Andrew could make out one of the metal frames on that tree as well.

He laughed to himself as he watched her. Most people thought of the deer as pests that ate the flowers and shrubs. Jill was encouraging them to come visit her.

What the hell? Might as well go say hey to pretty Jillie Walsh.

He drew a pair of threadbare jeans up over his hips and tossed a well-worn Yale sweatshirt over his t-shirt. Shoved his feet into a pair of duck boots and trotted downstairs without bothering to tie the laces of the boots. His grandmother's yard connected with the Walsh's by a fence in the main areas, but toward the back, where the yards became more wooded, the fence ended and the two yards were open to one another. Andrew trotted around the back end of the fence and headed toward Jill.

Before he reached her, he was greeted by Jill's dog, who ran up to Andrew as if the two of them were old friends. The dog jumped up with both paws on Andrew's chest to land kisses on his face.

"Hey, boy," Andrew said. He buried his hands in the curly fur to give the dog a good scratch before heading toward Jill.

Jill was headed back toward the house so Andrew called out to her as he fell into an easy jog. "Jill! Welcome back."

He watched as she turned toward him and squinted against the glare of the morning sun. She hesitated before returning his greeting. The dog ran back and forth between Jill and Andrew, bouncing as if he couldn't wait for them to meet up in the middle.

"Andrew? Wow, is that really you?"

"Yeah. I heard you were back in town. Saw you out here and thought I'd say hi before breakfast," Andrew explained as he approached her.

Jill let out a laugh. "Breakfast? It's almost ten thirty. You're just having breakfast?"

Andrew shrugged. "I've been sleeping in lately."

He had no problem getting up at six o'clock on days he went to the office, but easily reverted to sleeping later on weekends and vacations when he felt like it.

Jill tilted her head and studied him. "You're living at your grandmother's?"

"Uh, just for a while," he said vaguely, not sure if Nora would want him to mention her hip. Nora was proud and might not want everyone to know how much help she needed right now. "I'm taking a leave of absence from work for a while."

"Um, I was just going to make some hot chocolate." She

gestured over her shoulder toward the house. "Do you want some?"

"Sure."

Andrew eyed Jill sideways as they walked toward the house together. He couldn't believe how incredible she looked with her cheeks all red from the cold and her hair tangled up around the collar of her coat. Andrew was dying to see what she looked like when all the layers of winter clothing were stripped off.

Most of the women he dated wore ridiculously tiny coats and gloves made for fashion, not warmth. Jill was bundled up in an old, bulky ski jacket and still looked better than any of those women.

She had very little makeup on, but her eyes sparkled and Andrew found he couldn't look away from them as the two of them talked. Jill Walsh still had the same appeal, and he still responded. More so now as a man who'd experienced women than he had as a fifteen-year-old boy with only his imagination to fuel him.

He shook off his thoughts. She was his grandmother's neighbor and Andrew knew his grandmother was still friends with Jill's grandparents. In his book, that meant she was off limits. He didn't date women that close to home.

Jill opened the door and stomped the snow off her boots. He watched with interest as she stripped off her coat and crossed to the stove to turn on a burner. Yup. Incredible body, just like he figured. Damn, what a waste. Why did the woman who was so strictly off limits have to be so damn gorgeous?

"Nora said you're a photographer now," Andrew's voice was husky. He tried to control his response and pulled his boots off before grabbing a stool at the kitchen island.

"Mmm hmm. It started out as mostly a hobby but now I'm trying to make it work fulltime."

"What do you photograph? Do you do portraits and things or...?" His voice trailed off and his gaze moved to Jill's slender fingers as she added marshmallows to a mug of steaming hot chocolate and handed it to him.

How the hell can fingers be sexy?

Andrew knew the answer to that. They were sexy because he pictured those fingers on him. Running over his chest, digging into his shoulders, wrapping around his...damn. Now he was aroused.

Baseball stats. Old women doing aerobics in their underwear. The square root of 759 is...27.55. No, 27.54. It helped to be good with numbers.

"I photograph nature, mostly. Occasionally, people or pets, but mostly nature and wildlife. I got lucky and found a couple of galleries that exhibit my work. Now I'm working with a marketing group here to set up an online store for prints, gift cards, that sort of thing."

"I'd like to see some of your work sometime," Andrew said, but he noted that Jill looked hesitant. She seemed almost shy about discussing her work, and she didn't offer to show him any pieces.

Jill watched Andrew over her mug, and made idle small talk with him about New Haven but her heart rate was going a mile a minute. She couldn't take her eyes off him. That dirty blond hair that was just a tad too long. Scruffy chin and strong jaw. And, those eyes.

Those eyes that that were so steamy and sinful, they made her feel like she could melt into a puddle at his feet if she didn't look away.

Just last night she had wondered what he would be like all grown up, and here he was in the flesh, as if her thoughts had conjured him out of thin air.

And oh, what incredible flesh his was. Jill had guessed

Andrew would be good looking as an adult, but good looking didn't begin to describe the perfect model of manliness sitting before her.

She casually let her eyes drop to his chest and was amazed at the hard expanse of it, evident under the snug fit of the sweatshirt he wore. Andrew's jeans hugged lean hips and long legs and she suspected there wouldn't be an ounce of fat under those clothes.

The soft, faded material of his jeans tugged tightly across his thighs as he raised his feet onto the rungs of his kitchen stool. Jill swallowed a groan and dragged her eyes away from his lap. Except her gaze caught on other parts of his lap as she tried to pull away and she couldn't prevent the quick glance at his zipper or the imagined images of what lay beneath it.

Crappity, crap, crap. Stop looking, Jill!

She forced her eyes up, but even that was problematic. Just the sight of his hands when he accepted the mug sent Jill's mind reeling in naughty directions. She shivered when his hand brushed hers and wondered what those strong hands would feel like on her skin, around her waist, or skimming up to her breasts. She blushed and had difficulty drawing her eyes to his face.

What was wrong with her? She almost cringed to think she was sitting in her grandparents' kitchen thinking about a naked Andrew Weston.

I must be more overdue for a meaningless fling than I thought, Jill mused as she watched him wink at her over his mug. On so many men, a wink like that would look like such as arrogant gesture. For Andrew, it just looked easy and sexy. Just part of who he was.

She wondered if she could sleep with him. He sure seemed to be laid back and not exactly Mr. Commitment, which boded well for a casual fling.

On the other hand, Andrew was too close to home to mess around with. Their families were close. Things would be uncomfortable down the road when they had to see each other after it ended. Probably not wise to mess with him, even if he was a Greek god brought to life in her kitchen. She buried a sigh and focused on friendly chit chat instead of sexy fantasies.

CHAPTER 5

Andrew wandered toward the back of the 26th floor of the Sutton Capital building. It was quiet with many of the staff out to lunch. He said hi to a few people as he moved through the floor, but he was hoping Jack was in his office.

On his way to his friend's office, though, he passed Roark Walker, head of Suttons legal department and a close family friend of Jack's deceased parents.

The older man with the close-cropped white hair and dark skin greeted Andrew with a warm handshake and hug. "How's your grandmother? I told Mrs. Poole we should bake something for her and bring it by but she's fighting me on it."

Andrew grinned. He didn't tell Roark that Jack's housekeeper had already brought muffins by the house for Nora.

Roark spent more and more time lately at Jack's house with Mrs. Poole. The two had an odd relationship. Andrew would swear Roark was half in love with Mrs. Poole but she spent most of her time scowling and snapping at him. Which was odd for a woman who treated most of the people in her world like they were family whether she'd known them for five minutes or five years.

"Nora's doing well," Andrew said. "Frustrated at being stuck in the house." That was putting it mildly. Nora didn't do bed-bound well.

Roark jerked a head over his shoulder. "You'll find your boys out on the terrace."

Andrew smiled. The older man always called Jack, Chad, and Andrew 'the boys.'

"Thanks, Roark. I'm sure Nora would love a visit if you have time."

Roark nodded. "I'll make a point to see her soon."

Andrew kept going and wove through the desks that filled the main office space for the administrative staff and walked to the doors to the outdoor garden terrace that had become an ad hoc employee lounge. One of the human resources staff had nestled bistro tables and chairs among the foliage and there was now a sitting area with overstuffed outdoor armchairs and a firepit.

The firepit was rarely lit, but they occasionally set it up and sometimes even roasted marshmallows out there after hours. It made working late on big projects more enjoyable if you could take a break for gooey marshmallows and melted chocolate sandwiches.

Jack and Chad were sitting in two of the armchairs, feet propped on the unlit firepit.

Andrew went through the glass doors and grinned at their surprise. He hadn't told them he'd be swinging by.

Jack tilted his head at a chair. "Sit. We're being lazy while the staff isn't around to see it."

Andrew had to laugh as he sank into the chair. These two were the least lazy people he knew. Though, everyone had noticed Jack had started cutting back on his hours in the office when he married Kelly.

He still worked weekends and late nights when he absolutely had to but he no longer showed up before six am and left after eight at night.

"How's Nora doing?" Chad asked.

"Stubborn is how she's doing." Andrew scowled as the other two men grinned at his response.

"She doesn't want to do her physical therapy," he said, "so I have to stand there every time the therapist comes to the house and remind Nora that we can check her into a residential rehab center if she doesn't do the work. You would think after having that conversation three times a week for two weeks, she'd get it and we could be done with it."

The men were laughing, but Chad glanced at the doors, his face going grim.

"Listen, as long as we're here, I wanted to talk to you guys about Sam."

Samantha Page was currently on leave from Sutton Capital while she worked for the FBI but they were hoping she'd come back when she was finished.

"How's she doing?" Jack asked, sitting up and putting his arms on his legs as he leaned forward. "Any better?"

Chad shook his head. "Not unless crying on the couch as she watches the Wizard of Oz is better."

Andrew cursed under his breath.

Samantha had come to work for them shortly after Chad took over security at Sutton when he'd finished out his last tour with the Army Rangers. She was a brilliant hacker who really could be doing more with her mind than working for them, but she and Chad had hit it off and she seemed to have found a place at the company.

Sam was socially awkward and quirky as hell, but to them, that was all the more reason to be there for her when she needed them. She wouldn't reach out for help. She'd sit at home and try to handle what was happening on her own.

And since what she was doing for the FBI was related to Kelly's kidnapping earlier that year, they all wanted to be sure she got through it.

"Will she talk to you about it?" Jack asked.

Chad lifted a shoulder. "To the extent she can. We had a conversation about a hypothetical woman who was helping the FBI track down women kidnapped and sold into slavery by a kidnapping ring. The gist of it was that Sam's found five of the twelve women they know about and they've been rescued along with several other women they found during the operations."

"Hypothetically," Andrew said.

Chad gave a nod. "I told her its important for her to focus on the fact she got those women home and that's a lot more than anyone could have hoped for. Most women who are sold like that don't ever get out. But you guys know Samantha. She's beating herself up that she hasn't been able to track the others. This kind of work is hard on her."

"Will she see someone about it?" Andrew asked.

Chad nodded. "She says she will. I'm going to speak to a friend of mine who works with former veterans and see if he has a recommendation for someone she can see about all this."

"Good," Jack nodded. "I'll go by and see her soon, let her know we're all here for whatever she needs."

They could hear the office beginning to fill up as people returned from lunch and the buzz of conversation filtering out onto the patio also meant people would be able to hear them.

Andrew stood, making a mental note to call Sam when he could. Maybe he'd see if she'd done any more work on her multi-player online game she was designing. He didn't play them, but she'd told him about the world she was building one day at lunch and it sounded pretty freaking amazing. And that kind of creativity would probably be good for her right about now.

"Hey, Kelly and I are going to get drinks with a friend of hers after work today. You guys want to swing by?"

Chad shook his head. "Can't make it tonight."

Andrew shrugged. "I can." He grinned. "I don't have to wake up in the morning for work."

Jack and Chad only rolled their eyes at him as he lifted a hand in a lazy wave and left them to get back to work.

∼

Andrew walked into the bar in downtown New Haven and immediately saw Jack and Kelly. They sat at a tall bar table at the end of the long room. When Andrew approached, Kelly hopped down off the stool and hugged him.

Jack and Kelly were married last May to ensure Jack remained CEO of his father's company, Sutton Capital. They remarried in August after they fell in love during a whirlwind romance that took everyone, including them, by surprise.

Andrew had been happy to discover he really liked having Kelly around. She was a sister in the same way Jack felt like a brother. He loved them both and was more than happy they'd found each other. Still, at times lately, Andrew had pangs of jealousy for the life Jack had found with Kelly.

Andrew had fallen in love once before and discovered just how dangerous it was to share such intimate feelings with someone. The woman he loved had betrayed Andrew's love. Had also taken money from Andrew's parents in the process and the deception left him crushed and reeling from the blow.

He didn't doubt he might fall in love again someday, but he would have a problem revealing that love if he did. There was no way he wanted to make himself that vulnerable again. He just couldn't imagine putting himself in that position, even if that meant he could never have what Jack and Kelly shared.

Pushing that regret aside once again, Andrew smiled at the happy couple in front of him.

"What's the special occasion?" Andrew hadn't seen much of them since he'd taken the leave of absence to get Nora settled in at home. He was glad to have the excuse to get out and see them.

Their grins were huge as Kelly spilled the news. "We're having a baby!"

Jack pulled Kelly to him, wrapping his arms around her from the back, his hands settling on her still flat tummy. The look on his face said it all. Andrew didn't think he'd ever seen his friend this happy. And that made him happy.

"Aw, Kels, that's great!" Andrew pulled Kelly in for a bear hug and kissed her cheek. He grasped Jack's hand in a shake that turned into one of those one-armed man hugs.

"Gonna be one lucky kid, guys," Andrew said.

He meant it, despite the sting of loss he always felt when he thought about kids. Jack and Kelly were two of the best people he knew. He and Jack were at Yale together years ago and he knew Jack would make a great dad.

He might not have known Kelly long, but anyone who knew her for even a short time knew she was kind and generous. She was a special person.

"The baby's due in June," Kelly's smile grew. "We're not telling anyone other than family and you right now, though, because I'm still in my first trimester, so keep it quiet."

"You got it," Andrew grinned.

Jack handed Andrew a beer and the two men clinked their bottles in a silent toast.

Kelly's excitement was contagious. Jack caught Andrew's eye and gave him a silent look, asking him if he was okay with their news. Jack was one of a very select group of people who knew how painful news of babies and children could be to Andrew. Andrew gave him a slight nod and smiled. He didn't want Jack worrying about his feelings at a time like this.

"By the way, one of my friends is meeting us here tonight," Kelly said. There was a hint of mischief in her tone. "She's gorgeous and super talented. She just moved to town a little while ago and wants to meet more people. I thought she might like meeting you."

Her smile had matchmaker written all over it.

Jack mouthed 'sorry' to Andrew behind Kelly's back but

Andrew barely registered the words. His mind flashed to an image of Jill sipping hot cocoa in her grandmother's kitchen. For some reason, he wasn't really in the mood to meet another woman, no matter how perfect the woman may be.

Andrew briefly wondered what that was about before he excused himself to go to the bathroom. He needed to get away from there and clear his head before Kelly went any further with her plan.

Jack turned to Kelly as soon as Andrew was out of earshot. "Hon, you realize he's pretty committed to bachelorhood, right?"

Kelly brushed off Jack's warning. "Nonsense. That man wants to be married just as much as you did when I found you. He's just as clueless about it, too."

Jack let out a bark of laughter. It was true he hadn't had a clue that he was looking for love and marriage when he and Kelly began their marriage. He'd been completely caught off guard when he fell head over heels in love, but he could honestly say he'd never been happier in his life.

But Andrew's story was very different from Jack's and Jack knew it would take a hell of a lot for Andrew to ever trust a woman again.

"No, sweetheart, he really doesn't. Andrew has three categories of women in his world. Nora and Lydia are family. He trusts them and loves them. Then there are his friends. Andrew has lots of friends and many of them are female, but they're just that: friends and nothing more. Ever. He lets them get to know him and he probably trusts them on some level, but he never dates them.

"His third category would be the women he has arrangements with. They're women he sleeps with and nothing more. They're not girlfriends. He doesn't trust them. He doesn't let them get to know him. He doesn't build relationships with them. And he never, ever mixes any of those worlds. We don't meet the women he sleeps with. If he needs a date for a work function, he brings a friend. Never a real date. I know that's hard for you to understand, Kelly, but he needs it that way. It's just the way he is, honey."

Kelly's face fell and she frowned at Jack. "That can't be. Why would anyone live like that? Why wouldn't he even introduce the women he's with to you and Chad? You're his best friends."

"Chad and I are used to it. Andrew was hurt once and he didn't get over what happened. Hell, it was bad. None of us expected him to be able to get over it, so we don't take it personally that he's like this. I know you want to change him, Kels, but you can't. You gotta let him be who he is."

Kelly shook her head. "But why? What happened to him?"

Jack knew Kelly's heart was in the right place and he hated to have to disappoint her. He looked over his shoulder in the direction Andrew had gone. "I'll tell you when we get home."

Jack didn't think Andrew would mind if he told Kelly, but he wanted to give Andrew a heads up first.

"Oh, there's Jill," Kelly said as she looked over Jack's shoulder to the door of the bar. "It can't be as bad as you say. You'll see. He'll like Jill."

Kelly looked so hopeful, Jack just let it go.

Kelly raised her hand to wave her friend over. Jack turned to see a good-looking blond woman headed their way. She was older than Kelly. Jack estimated the woman to be closer to Jack's and Andrew's ages of thirty-three and she was, without a doubt, Andrew's type. Blond and petite with an open smile.

Even so, Jack worried that Jill and Kelly might have higher expectations for a relationship than Andrew would be able to give. He also knew there wasn't going to be any way to stop Kelly once she set her mind on something, and apparently, right now, she wanted to set up these two.

Jill smiled and shook hands with Jack when Kelly introduced him as her husband.

"Jack's best friend, Andrew, will be back in a minute. Did I mention him to you earlier?" Kelly asked Jill.

Kelly's effort at nonchalance was clear, but the setup was obvious and Jill had to fight not to cringe. She didn't know if she was ready for this.

"Andrew is the Chief Financial Officer of Jack's company and he's ridiculously smart and good looking. *Really* good looking." Kelly ignored Jack's 'hey!' at her description of Andrew.

Jill's mind flashed to Andrew Weston in his faded jeans and old sweatshirt. A far cry from the guy Kelly was describing, but he'd been on Jill's mind since the morning he'd come over to say hello.

"He's a really fun guy, too. I think you'll like him." Kelly smiled.

"Uh," Jill hesitated. "I don't really think I'm looking for a relationship right now, Kelly. I was thinking I'd just take a break, you know?" *Except for fantasizing about my hot-as-hell neighbor.* Jill pictured Andrew's lazy sex-charged smile and shivered with pleasure.

But then, there he was. Andrew Weston was right in front of her, in the flesh, coming up beside Kelly with that wide, sexy smile on his face.

"Jill! What are you doing here?" He asked before she could close her mouth.

She probably looked like an idiot, drooling over him.

Kelly and Jack turned to Andrew as one. "You guys know each other?"

Jill blushed but Andrew explained, "Jill lives next door to my grandmother. She used to visit her grandparents when they lived there years ago and now she's back. I was crazy in love with her when I was fifteen and used to watch her out by her grandparents' pool," Andrew said as he winked at Jill.

She felt her face turn five shades redder than it already was as she tried to laugh with everyone else at Andrew's comment. Hopefully he couldn't tell the tables were turned and she was the one with the ridiculously hopeless crush on him this time.

"What do you want to drink?" Andrew asked her. He moved around Jack and Kelly to stand next to Jill and she had to force herself not to read anything into his move.

Andrew Weston is off limits. Andrew Weston is off limits.

Maybe if Jill repeated the mantra enough, her body would catch onto what her brain knew. Yes, she'd thought briefly about a fling with him, but he was too close to home to do that. His grandmother was good friends with her grandparents. Not to mention he was apparently good friends with the husband of the only friend she had in town.

She focused instead on the shock of finding out that Andrew wasn't the lazy bum she thought he was. Apparently he didn't just live off his grandmother's wealth and sleep the day away. How was it possible that he was the CFO of Jack's company and, according to Kelly, incredibly smart and successful? Jill had him pegged as some playboy socialite.

Andrew ran his hand down the small of Jill's back sending a deliciously wicked thrill through her and leaned in close to her ear. "Do you want something to drink, Jill?"

She realized she hadn't answered Andrew when he asked her the first time. His hand on her back was probably completely innocent and meant to be friendly, but the heat that radiated through her at his touch was anything but innocent – and was very distracting. She looked up at him and swallowed. Trying to get the gears in her mind to kick in and function.

"A margarita?" Jill suggested but in her head she was doing all she could to try to shut down the effect of Andrew's touch. *It's gonna be a loooong night.*

CHAPTER 6

*A*ndrew couldn't believe Kelly had been trying to set him up with Jill. Unfortunately, that connection was all the more reason for him to stay away from his sexy neighbor, romantically. Her family was not only literally and figuratively close to his, she was also friends with his friends now. Way too close to home for Andrew's comfort. Too bad she was so damned tempting.

He walked back over to the group with Jill's drink in his hand and listened as Kelly explained that she and Jill met recently at a gallery in town. Jill had been there overseeing the installation of her photographs when Kelly went in to shop.

"Her work is amazing. I went in to look for something to put in the living room over the fireplace and couldn't believe her photographs. I bought one of her pieces for that spot and another smaller piece for your study, Jack," Kelly was saying.

"I didn't realize one of the galleries you show in is here in New Haven," Andrew said. He handed Jill her margarita and watched her take a sip.

He found himself staring at her lips as they caressed the rim of the glass then swallowed a groan when her tongue came out to lick the salt off her full lips.

When he reluctantly tore his eyes away and brought them back up to Jill's, she answered his question. Damn, she was going to be hard to ignore.

"One is here in New Haven and the other's in Hartford. I'll be meeting with a third gallery in New York next week and I'm hoping they'll offer me a temporary installation on a trial basis," Jill said.

"Well, you'll need to show me your work soon," Andrew heard himself say, and he resisted the urge to smack himself in the head.

Bad idea, Andrew. A private showing of Jill's art sure as hell wasn't going to cool things off.

The group talked and laughed. Jack told stories about Andrew from business school and Kelly told Jill about her first year in law school.

Andrew noticed that Jill seemed to be sucking down quite a few margaritas. He wondered if she was in a bit of a wild phase after her divorce or if she was always like this.

As he watched her, Andrew found himself wondering a lot of things about Jill. What happened with Jill and her husband? Did he cheat on her? Hurt her? Obviously, he was a fucking moron for letting her slip away. Complete fucking moron.

There were other things going through his head, too. Things that sure as hell shouldn't be there. He wondered what Jill looked like under the green sweater she wore. The green sweater that made her hazel eyes look a bit deeper than they usually did. What would it feel like to kiss those full, rose-colored lips? How would she respond during sex? With little moans and pants or would she scream out his name?

Oh shit. I'm a dead man.

"Andrew? Andrew?" Kelly asked.

"Hmm? Oh! Sorry. What was that, Kelly?"

Nice recovery, asshole.

"We were just saying that it's probably time for us to call it a night. You okay?" Jack asked.

"Yeah, I was just thinking about some work things. I should head home, too," Andrew said. They stood and prepared to leave. He noticed Jill didn't seem all that steady on her feet when she slid off the barstool and picked up her purse.

"Why don't I drive you home, Jill?" Andrew took hold of Jill's arm to steady her and she smiled up at him.

"I think I had too many margaritas," she whispered at a volume that let the whole group hear her confession.

Andrew laughed. "I think you might be right." He turned to Jack and Kelly. "I'll get her home, guys. I'll be back in the office next week, Jack."

"You sure you're ready?" Jack asked Andrew.

"Yeah. I've got Nora settled in at home and the nurses seem to have things under control. I'm going to stay in the carriage house a while longer in case she needs me around, but I'm ready to get back to work. Being a bum for a couple of weeks was fun, but I'm bored."

"What happened to Nora?" Jill frowned.

"Oh, uh. She fell on some ice and broke her hip. That's why I'm staying there for a while. I wanted to get Nora and Lydia more help at the house and set up nurses for her so she can recover at home instead of in a rehab center," he explained.

"Ha! I thought you were a bum who partied all day and lived off your grandmother," Jill said.

Jack and Kelly started to laugh while Andrew looked down at Jill and scowled.

"Why would you think that?"

"You came wandering over at 10:30 in the morning and it was obvious you had just woken up, hadn't shaved in days... You said you were 'taking a leave of absence' and you were sleeping in Nora's carriage house. I thought 'leave of absence' meant you were living off her. What else would I think?" Jill asked.

Jack and Kelly continued to laugh at Andrew, who was anything but a lazy bum. Even Andrew cracked a smile as he steered Jill outside to his Aston Martin and settled her safely into the front seat.

As they drove home, Andrew realized just how drunk Jill was when she started to slur and babble. She talked about the snow and the trees covered in ice as they drove on the small New England highway that took them from New Haven to Westbrook.

He had a feeling she didn't get this drunk very often. When they were close to home, she turned in her seat and studied him through sleepy eyes.

"So, you're really not a bum? You're like this huge financial wizard and you have a big career. Nora's not supporting you?"

"Nope." he grinned at Jill and wondered why this revelation seemed so significant to her. "I'm really not. I'm a grown up with my own place and everything. Does that bother you?"

She sighed and turned back to the front windshield as Andrew steered them toward home. "It just confirmed that you really, really, really can't be my rebound guy," she said with a drunken little wave of her hand.

This brought a huge grin from Andrew. "Oh, yeah? You wanted me to be your rebound guy?" *Hell, yes!*

He kept one eye on the road and glanced over at Jill.

She must have been very drunk because she didn't hesitate to spill the beans as he pulled the car down the driveway of her grandparents' house. Andrew turned off the engine when he reached the house.

"Of course. You're hot. But you're also Nora's grandson so that makes you a bad idea. A verrrry bad idea. When I thought you were kind of a bum, it might have been okay to have a fling, but now you're not, so it isn't." Jill babbled on, making it a little hard for Andrew to follow her logic, but he mostly understood where she was coming from.

Still, he was surprised to hear her frank assessment of their relationship possibilities. Or rather, lack thereof.

He watched in bemused shock as his sexy-as-hell neighbor explained that she couldn't sleep with him even though she wanted to because he was friends with her friend and he was the son of her grandparents' friend. Too complicated.

Andrew laughed at Jill as she finished her speech. Since he also knew getting involved was a bad idea, he didn't argue with her. He wanted to argue, though.

He wanted to find some reason to say she was wrong and it would be perfectly fine for them to sleep together. That's what his body wanted, but his brain still had some control, thankfully. He leaned across the seat toward her, breathing in the incredible mixture of scents he had come to identify with Jill.

"I know what you mean, sweet Jill," he whispered, as he undid her seatbelt. "I know just what you mean."

With a great deal of effort, Andrew pulled back before Jill's proximity got the better of him. He opened his car door and jogged around and opened her door. With all the control he could muster, he walked a rather dazed looking Jill up to her front door, helped her inside, and went home to the second cold shower that Jill had inspired in just a few days.

CHAPTER 7

Jill lay in her bed reliving the conversation from her ride home with Andrew last night. She cringed as the memory of her words came back to her all too clearly. She never thought she'd wish for a nice little blackout.

Oh. My. Peanuts.

I actually told Andrew Weston I wanted to have rebound sex with him. What was I thinking?

She hadn't been thinking. She had been drunk. Jill rarely drank more than a glass of wine when she went out. She certainly never had to be driven home or spilled her guts to her steamy next-door neighbor because she over indulged. She wasn't the type.

But, for some reason, last night Jill had just wanted to acknowledge her attraction to the one man who couldn't be her rebound guy. Now she wanted to erase the images she'd created in her head of sharing a bed with Andrew.

With a groan, Jill rolled over and shut her eyes against the sun and the memories of the most embarrassing encounter she'd ever had. What would she do when she ran into Andrew again? How would she face her neighbor after what she had blurted out the night before?

Jill's husband had left her feeling humiliated and insecure. Now those feelings were magnified by the added mortification of having thrown herself at her handsome neighbor.

Despite her embarrassment, one other thing stuck in her mind from the night before. She remembered the way she felt when Andrew leaned over to unbuckle her seat belt. His body so close to hers. His breath brushing against her neck as he leaned into her. Jill closed her eyes and tried to will the images out of her head.

Crap.

It wasn't working. Those images weren't going anywhere anytime soon.

~

Andrew slept a little later than usual, but he woke with a smile on his face. Sweet, sexy Jill wanted him to be her rebound guy. His smile grew wider at the thought.

He had a feeling Jill might regret blurting out her fantasy about him and her confession sure as hell didn't make it any easier for him to stay away from her. In a way, Andrew almost wished she hadn't told him she was interested in him.

Although they were both in agreement being together couldn't happen, knowing Jill wanted the same thing he did would make keeping their relationship platonic that much harder.

He showered and dressed in sweats and an old t-shirt then tossed on his gym shoes and a fleece pullover, trying to keep his mind away from thoughts of Jill. He was meeting Chad – Jack's cousin and the head of Security at Sutton Capital – at the gym to play basketball at noon. Before leaving the house, Andrew went to the window and looked outside to see if Jill was around. He didn't see her out in the yard but he figured she must be up. It was already eleven o'clock.

Grabbing a few bottles of water and some aspirin, he grinned as he made his way down the stairs and out to his car. He tossed his gym bag in the back seat and pulled the car down Nora's drive, then back up the driveway next door.

He stood on Jill's front porch with the water and aspirin in hand, ringing her bell. She probably wouldn't want to see him first thing, when she was likely waking up with a hangover but he didn't care. Call him a masochist for wanting to see an attractive woman he couldn't have as more than a friend, but he wanted to see her again.

The door swung open and Andrew's smile widened. How the hell did Jill manage to look so damn sexy in sweats and a tank top with her hair all messed up and her eyes barely open?

"Morning, sunshine," he said with a grin. He watched Jill's eyes widen with the realization he was on her doorstep.

"Morning," Jill mumbled as her face took on a crimson hue.

"Just came to help you with your hangover." With his smile firmly in place, he handed her the container of painkillers and the bottled water.

"*Ugh*. I don't think I've done this much damage to my body since college." She took the water and pills out of Andrew's hands.

"Take those, drink all the water, and get some sleep," Andrew said as he turned toward his car. He turned back, remembering Jack and Kelly were hosting a party the following night. "Are you going to Jack and Kelly's house tomorrow night?"

"If this headache goes away by then, yes," Jill said.

"Ride together?"

"Sure," Jill nodded and smiled.

"Great," Andrew smiled. "I'll pick you up at seven."

CHAPTER 8

Jennie groaned as she walked into the locker room of the gym on the fifth floor of the Sutton Capital Building. It helped that Kelly held the door for her, but even so, each step felt like torture.

"I'm never letting you talk me into that again."

Kelly only grinned at her.

"I mean it." Jennie sank onto the bench between lockers and eyed her best friend. "That man pushes hard. Do you always workout with him?"

This brought a laugh from Kelly. "No, we usually just do self-defense sessions together but he's decided I need to up my cardio."

Zach Harris was apparently a Jack-of-all-trades. He'd been hired by Kelly's husband as her bodyguard after she was kidnapped, but he was also teaching her self-defense. And now he'd seemingly added trying to run her butt into the ground to the mix.

They'd just done enough time on a stair machine to make Jennie puke.

She laid back on the bench, bringing her feet up to balance

on it like a bed. Not that it was anywhere near as comfortable as a bed, but hey, she was at least lying down now.

Kelly started pulling clean clothes from her locker, but she looked over her shoulder, talking as she did.

"Are you coming to our house tonight?"

Jennie threw an arm over her eyes, blocking out the overhead lights. "If I survive until then."

Kelly laughed, but sobered. "Have you been to see Sam? I called to see if she was coming but she hasn't called me back. I'm worried about her."

Jennie sat up, frowning. "Me, too. Chad went to see her and I stopped by the other day. She's not working at all."

Kelly shot Jennie an alarmed look. "You know she'll never lose her job. She'll have a place at Sutton whenever she's ready to come back."

Jennie waved a hand. "I don't mean that. I mean on the stuff she loves. She's stopped working on her game. She's not sleeping much. I think she's depressed."

Kelly sat next to Jennie. "I wonder if she'd see a therapist. I like mine a lot and I think talking to her is really helping me."

"You're seeing a therapist?"

Kelly nodded. "Hell yes. Zach has this whole program he does for when he's hired to guard someone who went through something traumatic like I did. He's your bodyguard, but he also teaches you self-defense and gets you hooked up with a therapist and stuff."

"Chad connected you and Jack with Zach, right?"

It was Kelly's turn to nod. "I think they knew each other because of their time in the military or something." Kelly scrunched her brows. "Or maybe it was through one of Chad's connections at the police force. Either way, he set us up with him."

Jennie focused on untying her sneakers and slipped them off. "Chad's a good man."

Kelly's "mm hmm" response contained a lot more meaning than the sound would let on.

Jennie looked at her and shook her head. Her friend was always trying to imply there was more between Jennie and Chad than there was. There so wasn't anything between them.

And there wouldn't be. Not if she had anything to say about it.

CHAPTER 9

Jill sat on the edge of her bed to pull on her boots as she got ready to go out for the evening. She had to stop thinking about Andrew as anything more than a friend, but no matter how rational she tried to be, logic didn't stop her body's reaction to him.

Even the thought that she would see him in a few minutes had her body flushed and heated, tingling in anticipation of seeing him again.

It had taken Jill an hour to choose what to wear. She wanted to look good for Andrew, but she didn't want to look like she was trying too hard.

In the end, she settled on a snug-fitting sweater dress. The dress came to mid-thigh and had a cowl neckline. It was a rich, reddish-brown color and the tan cowboy boots she slipped on complimented the sweater perfectly. The boots had teal blue accents etched into them and came to just below her knee. Teal earrings added a little flair.

When the doorbell rang, Jill met Rev at the front door where he was busy letting out excited barks every few seconds to try to hurry her along. The dog loved anyone who came to the house and was pretty sure they all came to visit him. Made a girl feel secure where burglaries were concerned.

Holding Rev back with one hand, she opened the door to let Andrew inside and smiled at him. When his eyes ran up and down her body in a heated appraisal she warmed. The way he looked had her feeling as if his hands were searing a pattern across her body rather than just his eyes.

She might not be able to have him but the way he treated her was beginning to do wonders for her battered and bruised confidence where men were concerned.

"You look amazing," Andrew said.

"Thanks." She smiled. *Definitely good for my confidence.* "I just need to get Rev's leash. Kelly wants him to play with her new puppy so we should probably drive my SUV instead of your car."

Jill had a feeling not many dogs had put their paws on the leather seats of Andrew's car.

He raised his eyebrows. "Yup, SUV it is," he said with a grin.

They led Rev out the front door. The dog bounded and Jill loaded him into her Explorer.

Andrew looked longingly at his car as they got into Jill's SUV. "I'm going to have to put Adelaide away tomorrow and get out the Tahoe. It's time for my winter car."

Jill laughed. "I don't know what's funnier. The fact that you have a winter car and a summer car, or the fact that you call your car Adelaide."

"What else would I call her? That's her name!" Andrew said, like the teenage boy she used to know.

She rolled her eyes and laughed at him, relaxing into the seat.

Andrew drove since he knew the way to Jack and Kelly's house and he and Jill slipped into a comfortable quiet on the way to the gathering. Rev sat straight up in one of the back seats and watched out the window as if he could somehow help with the navigation if he kept an eye on things.

When she and Andrew arrived thirty minutes later, Jill spotted Kelly and another woman playing with Kelly's new puppy. Andrew headed off to see Jack and Chad while she headed toward the women.

"Jill, you're here!" Kelly greeted Jill enthusiastically and then bent to pet Rev.

"Rev, this is my puppy Zoe. Zoe, this is Rev," Kelly said as she crouched down next to a fluffy black puppy who looked to be four or five months old. Who knew what breed of dog she was besides cute. She was the damned cute breed, that's what she was.

Rev laid down and rolled onto his side to allow the puppy to climb on him.

Zoe promptly began chewing Rev's ears as the two rolled together on the floor.

Jill smiled down at the dogs. "He's always so great with puppies. I don't know how he knows to lay down with them, but he always does. I can promise, I had nothing to do with him being such a great playmate. I'm pretty clueless when it comes to training."

Kelly grinned at Jill and then introduced her to the woman with the strawberry blond hair standing with them. "Jill, this is Jennie. Jennie – Jill. Jennie's dog, Zeke, has been on puppy duty all week so he was glad to have a break when I told her you'd bring Rev tonight."

They exchanged greetings and open smiles. "Do you also work at Sutton Capital, Jennie?"

Jennie and Kelly laughed, causing Jill to look at them quizzically, wondering what the inside joke was.

"Yes," Jennie explained. "I was Jack's temp secretary when I overheard him explaining to Andrew that his mom's will required Jack to be married by the time he was thirty-five. If he didn't marry within a week, he would lose a good portion of the shares of the company. I told Kelly what I had heard and she offered to marry him in exchange for her law school tuition."

Jill's jaw hit the floor as she gaped at Jennie and Kelly. "What? You married Jack for law school tuition?"

Kelly was completely unabashed as she responded with a huge smile on her face. "Yup! Sure did. We were supposed to be married for one year so he could satisfy the terms of his mother's will, but then we fell madly, completely in love with each other and the rest is history." Kelly sighed happily.

"I almost got fired for spying on Jack and telling Kelly his secret, but it was worth it." Jennie smiled broadly and launched into the story, telling Jill how Kelly walked into Jack's office and introduced herself to Jack's aunt and cousin as if she were Jack's fiancée. In reality, Jack and Kelly had never met before. Jill listened in awe as Jennie told her about the note Kelly passed to Jack that proposed the deal.

"Jack only accepted because he thought Andrew had sent Kelly to Jack to solve his problem. When Jack figured out Kelly hadn't been sent by Andrew, he pretty much freaked," Jennie said.

The girls laughed over the story that had ended in one of the most romantic marriages Jill had ever seen.

Kelly looked past Jennie's shoulder to where Chad stood talking to Christian Lang, a man who worked in tech services at Sutton.

"Chad can't keep his eyes off of you, Jen," Kelly said.

Jill casually turned to stand next to Kelly, leaning against a table so that it wasn't obvious she was trying to change her angle to look for Chad. "Which one is he?"

Jennie laughed. "He's the guy that looks like he could break any other man in this room in half with a flick of his wrist."

Jill scanned the room and quickly located the dark-haired god that stood about two inches taller than most of the men in the room. He looked a lot like Jack but his hair was darker and he was sheer muscle. Much larger than any other man there – that said something since there were a lot of really built men in the room, including Andrew.

Jill turned wide eyes to Kelly and Jennie. "Holy crap! He's like a truck."

Jennie grinned. "I know. I call him Tank if I want to get a rise out of him. Or the Hulk. He hates that one."

Kelly and Jill laughed. "Jennie likes to taunt the big, dangerous man. She's got a bit of a screw loose," Kelly explained.

The girls laughed and enjoyed another minute of ogling Chad before Kelly changed the subject.

"So, what's the story with you and Andrew?" Kelly asked. "And, don't try to tell me you just car-pooled here because you're neighbors. He hasn't taken his eyes off you all night."

Jill had been aware of Andrew's constant attention. She felt it every time he looked her way with tingling up her spine or heat racing to parts of her body she didn't want reacting to Andrew.

"Sorry to disappoint. Nothing is happening. Not that I can convince my body of that."

Kelly laughed and Jennie started fanning herself with one hand.

"Oh, I bet he could show you more than a little fun in the bedroom." Jennie laughed.

"No chance of anything happening?" Kelly asked.

"No, and I don't want it to. Our families know each other and we have mutual friends," Jill added with a pointed look at Kelly. "Neither of us is looking for anything serious so we don't want to have a casual relationship and then have to be a part of each other's lives after it ends. It would just be too weird."

"That sucks," Kelly said, "but I get what you mean. It's just too bad. Andrew's such a great guy and sooooo sexy. I thought you would be perfect for each other."

Jennie laughed and nodded. Before Jill could answer, Andrew

joined them, taking the spot right next to Jill. Her body came alive in response to him.

"Talking about me?" he asked.

Kelly and Jennie laughed and Jill felt her cheeks flush red. He leaned against the table next to Jill, and as he did his thigh brushed hers – just the slightest whisper of contact, but it sent edgy energy tripping through her body. She was instantly aroused.

"What is Andrew doing now, ladies?" Jack asked as he approached.

"Hey!" Andrew managed an indignant tone. "I just came to tell Jill I love the picture Kelly picked for over the fireplace in here."

The group turned toward the large print above the fireplace. It showed an ice-covered tree branch sparkling in the sun. Jill had taken the shot with the sun alighting on small droplets of water that fell to the ground as they melted from the branch. The scene was so simple, but the effect was mesmerizing.

Jill beamed at the compliment. "Thank you."

Jennie nodded. "It does look perfect in this room, Kelly. Just like you said it would. But you'll need to put something warmer in here for the spring and summer, though. You can pull this one back out each fall."

Jill grinned at Jennie's assessment. "That's the idea."

"God, that's brilliant," Andrew said, turning to Jill. "You're an artist and a business mogul. I never would have thought of seasonal art."

"It's beautiful," said a man who had joined the group shortly after Jack, but who hadn't been introduced to Jill yet. Jill felt his curiosity on her and smiled at him.

"Oh, sorry. Gabe, this is Jill Walsh." Jack made introductions. "She's the photographer I was telling you about." He turned to Jill.

"Jill, this is Gabriel Sawyer. He's an old friend of Chad's and mine. He owns a large chain of hotels and they're in the middle of redecorating about a third of them. Since you're getting more into the commercial side of things with some of your prints, I thought you might like to show him some of your work."

"I'd love to," said Jill. "I'd imagine you don't want anything seasonal, though."

"You're right, probably not seasonal, but I definitely want to see more of your work." Gabe smiled at her and Jill felt Andrew's body tense beside her.

She was surprised to find she liked the idea he might be jealous of Gabe, when really his jealousy should offend her. When her ex seemed jealous, it made Jill feel like a prized toy he didn't want anyone else to play with. With Andrew, it felt different, although she couldn't quite say how.

Still, she wasn't the kind of woman who would openly flirt with one man to make another jealous. She didn't play games like that.

But once again, his behavior was soothing something in her she hadn't thought could be soothed. And it felt good. Really good.

CHAPTER 10

*A*ndrew didn't think he had ever felt this crazed drive to be with a particular woman before. At least not since he'd left puberty behind. He enjoyed sex and had plenty of it, but even during his time with Blair, he never felt anything like the pull he felt from Jill.

Tonight, from across the room full of people, Jill's body called to his as though some unseen tether connected them, one that he couldn't break with distance or space. All night, Andrew had fought to keep sensuous images of Jill at bay. He tried walking away. He went to the other side of the room to mingle, but still she followed him in his thoughts.

Flashes of Jill's sexy legs, in those sweet cowboy boots, wrapped around his hips flew through his mind. Of burying his head in the soft curve of Jill's neck to breathe in the scent of her. Then lower, licking the sensitive swell of her breast. Closing his mouth around her nipple as she pushed her body closer to him, writhing for more.

Again, he had to shake off the images and force himself to focus on the party going on around him. He knew he couldn't date Jill. He never dated in his circle of friends. Hell, he never really dated. He slept with women.

Women who understood that he didn't want more from them. Women who knew he'd sleep with them a few times and then move on. No strings attached. No long-term relationship. Not even a friendship when it was over. Jill Walsh wasn't one of those women. Never could be.

He refocused on the group around him and saw Jill trying to hide a yawn behind her hand. He approached her and placed a hand on her lower back. When he leaned in to speak to her, he cursed himself for being weak enough to manufacture that small bit of contact. "You're tired. We can head home if you want."

She smiled up at him. "You caught that, huh?"

"It's all right. It's getting late. Even Rev and Zoe have quit." Andrew nodded at the dogs who were now asleep in a corner of the room.

"As long as you don't mind leaving, I'm ready to go."

"No problem." He turned to Jack and Kelly. "Hey guys, we're gonna head out. I'll see you Monday, Jack?"

"Thanks for coming you guys," Kelly said, hugging Andrew and then Jill.

Jack and Andrew said goodnight and several of the others in the small group of people that were left at the party called out good-byes as Jill, Andrew, and Rev made their way to the door.

Andrew was annoyed to see Gabe give Jill a card with his personal number scrawled on the back before they left. He wanted to growl and tell the hotel owner to back the hell off, but he managed to control the urge.

They rode in comfortable silence again. Neither felt the need to fill the gaps with talk and he liked that about her.

Before long Jill was asleep in the seat. His mind immediately went to thoughts of waking up with her next to him. He could almost feel her long, supple body pressed into his, arms and legs tangled, his body growing hard against her soft, giving curves...

Shit, where is this crap coming from? He didn't spend the whole night with women. There was no waking up next to them, no snuggling in bed with them, no pillow talk. Nothing. And it needed to stay that way.

Andrew turned his attention to the road and had them home in a few minutes, pulling Jill's Explorer up to her front door. God, she was so beautiful. He reached over and shook her slender shoulder gently.

"Jill, honey. We're home," he said softly, resisting the urge to wake her with kisses instead. He knew instinctively if he kissed the corner of her mouth and worked is way across her lips, she would wake and return his kiss.

What the fuck was happening to him? He wasn't that guy.

She woke slowly, looking around, trying to get her bearings. "Sorry. I guess I fell asleep."

"You were tired, huh? You should have told me you were so tired. We could have come home sooner," he said as he unbuckled his seatbelt and opened his door.

Jill got out of the car and opened the back door to let Rev jump out.

"It's okay. I was having fun. Besides, I'm my own boss. I can sleep as late as I want in the morning," she said with a smile.

He walked up to the front door with her and handed over the car keys. When their fingers brushed he let them linger for a moment, just a moment longer than he should have. The contact was small but the moment wasn't.

His eyes were stuck on hers and he knew if he wasn't careful, if he didn't stay in control, he would kiss her. His mind raced, debating the pros and cons, the danger of leaning in for just one taste of her.

Andrew stared at her lips and felt himself take a step closer until they stood only inches apart. Her mouth was so tempting. Those full, rosy lips begging him, pleading for just a brush of his tongue, a gentle nip from his teeth.

Rev sat in front of the unopened door and barked, breaking the moment. Thank God for small favors.

Well at least the dog has brains, since I'm apparently functioning with something else right now.

Head cleared, he took a step back, putting distance between him and Jill. "I guess Rev's ready for bed. Nite, Jill." His voice was husky with need but he hopped down off the porch and strode to his car.

Distance. It was the only thing that was going to save him now.

When he got in his car, he looked at her one last time. She stood watching him from the porch, fingertips touching her lips as if she too had wondered what that kiss would be like. As if she knew as well as he did that just one kiss would have the power to break their resolve.

He rolled down the window and smiled at her.

"Get some sleep, sweet Jill."

Then he forced himself to drive away.

CHAPTER 11

*A*lways a glutton for punishment, Andrew once again made the trek over to Jill's house the following morning. He was an idiot. Worse than an idiot. He seemed to have a sadistic masochistic streak he'd never realized was there.

He cut through the backyard, telling himself he was just going over to be friendly. He was being neighborly, that's all.

Andrew peeked in the kitchen window but didn't see Jill anywhere. There was a pan on the stove with eggs in it, though, and from the looks of it, they were well on their way to becoming burnt eggs.

He poked his head in the backdoor.

"Jill?" he called out. No answer.

He stepped into the kitchen and took the pan off the stove. Even Rev didn't make an appearance. Andrew stuck the pan on one of the cool burners, flicking off the hot one and walked toward the front of the house. He stopped mid stride in the hallway when he heard voices from the front entry.

Jill and someone else.

"Jake, I asked you for a clean break. I thought if I came to New Haven, you'd get the point. I don't want to see you. I don't want you checking up on me. *Or* dropping by to visit," Jill said.

Ex-husband, Jake? What the fuck is he doing here?
Andrew felt his body tense as he listened to the conversation. It wasn't any of his business. He should walk away, but the frustration in Jill's voice was evident. Frustration and something else. *Pain?*
Ah, shit. Andrew couldn't walk away and ignore that.
"Jill, don't be ridiculous. You just moved; you're starting over in a new city. You need me. There's no reason for you to be like this. We can be friends," a man's voice said.
"No. We really can't. That ship sailed when you slept with another woman. When you ended our marriage. When you moved in with her. There's not going to be any friendship, Jake."
Good. She was firm. The guy will get it and go away.
"You're being unreasonable, Jill," said the male voice.
Or not. Time's up, asshole.
Andrew stepped out into the entry.
"Hi, sweetheart," he said as he stepped up and put an arm around Jill. He felt her jump in surprise. "Who's this?"
The asshole at the door looked every bit as surprised as Jill to see him in the house.
"Um, uh," stammered Jill.
Andrew smiled at her, amused by the stunned look on her face. He was enjoying this way more than he should be.
He stuck out his hand to the ex standing on the doorstep. "Hi. I'm Andrew. You must be Jason. Wait, that's not right, John? Jarrod? What's his name, honey?" Andrew asked, turning back to look at Jill, who now appeared to understand his game plan.
"Jake. I'm her husband," Jake said.
Jill gasped audibly at the description and Andrew's amusement went out the window.
"I think you mean ex-husband. And I think Jill asked you to leave."
Andrew pulled her closer to him, snuggling her body against

his as he kept his gaze firmly on Jake. The man looked like he might argue for a second or two but then backed down.

"Fine. Jill, I'll talk to you soon," Jake said tightly as he turned on his heel and walked down the front steps.

Andrew slammed the door with a little more force than was probably necessary but it felt really good. Turning Jill in his arms, he studied her face. She still wore the same stunned, confused look. Damn, she felt so good in his arms. So right pressed up against his body.

"Sorry, I probably should have let you handle that. It just didn't sound like he was gonna leave any time soon and your eggs were burning," Andrew said.

Fuck he probably shouldn't have presumed to jump in there and handle that for her. He was almost as big a dick as her ex. She was handling it and he should have let her do that. Should have respected her.

But why should she have to handle everything on her own when he was there to support her?

He couldn't seem to let Jill go. The bewildered look on her face was just too damn cute.

"My eggs? Oh! My eggs. Oh, crap!" She broke out of his hold and rushed back to the kitchen, leaving Andrew with a disturbingly empty feeling where she'd been.

He walked into the kitchen to find Jill dumping eggs in the garbage can.

"I hate that he still gets me flustered. But, what the hell is he doing showing up this early in the morning, unannounced, now that I live forty minutes away from him. Who does that?"

She looked up at Andrew as if she expected him to be able to explain her ex's behavior.

"You handled him just fine. You stood your ground and told him to go away. I wouldn't call that flustered." Andrew watched as Rev tried to get into the garbage can for the trashed eggs.

"I tell him that every time he comes around. So far, the words are completely ineffective."

Andrew watched her crack more eggs into a bowl and begin to scramble them as he tried to figure out how to ask his next question.

"When you say he doesn't listen, you don't mean... I mean, he doesn't ever force his way in, does he?" He could feel the tightness in his jaw as he asked the question. He clenched his fists at his sides, holding his breath as he waited for Jill to answer.

She busied her hands with cooking the eggs as he waited and tried not to let his fury at the thought of her ex-husband pushing his way in, or worse, show.

"No, no. Nothing like that. He just doesn't listen, you know? What I don't get is why he keeps coming around. He's the one who left." Jill gestured Andrew toward the kitchen island as she slid scrambled eggs onto two plates. "Here, you earned breakfast."

She smiled and pulled two pieces of toast from the toaster, buttering them and placing one on her plate and one on Andrew's.

He was quiet for a minute while he thought about Jill's question.

"Only two reasons he'd keep coming around," he said slowly. "Either he really is an arrogant ass who thinks you can't live without him or he still wants to sleep with you."

Her head shot up. "What? No! I mean, no. He's...he left me. He's living with his mistress. He doesn't want... I mean, we don't. He's not..."

He laughed. "Okay, then he's an arrogant ass who thinks you can't live without him."

Jill frowned at her eggs. "Well, yes. Actually, that sounds exactly like him."

They ate the rest of their breakfast in silence. Jill seemed to be a million miles away and Andrew was busy having a little internal conversation with his dick about its reaction to Jill in her pajamas.

She wore men's pajama bottoms and a thin cami top that beautifully outlined the round curve of her breasts and hard peaks of her nipples.

If Andrew expected to keep his head around his tempting new friend, he really had to stop coming around first thing in the morning. Jill in pajamas with her hair mussed from sleep was way too tempting.

∼

Andrew walked into Jack's office for their morning meeting and found Chad and Jack were already there drinking coffee, waiting for him.

"Sorry, guys. Got a late start this morning," he said as he picked up the coffee that waited for him in front of his usual chair.

"No problem. We don't have much to go over today. A few details for the investors we have coming in and someone who's looking for a spot on your team, Andrew. Chad, you have anything else to go over?"

"Just a few employee raises," Chad said. This earned him puzzled looks from Jack and Andrew.

"We don't need to review raises for your people. We never have before," Andrew said.

He watched Chad squirm, not something you normally see from a guy like Chad, and instantly Andrew knew this had something to do with Jennie.

Chad was head over heels in love with Jennie, but she reported to Chad. In Chad's mind, that meant she was off limits. It also made him anal about being objective where she was concerned.

"One of them is Jennie's. I want you guys to review and

approve all of the raises so there's no question about... Well, you know," Chad finished, trying to act casual about his nervousness where Jennie was concerned.

"Aw, look at the big guy, Jack. He's growing up so fast...all hot for a girl," Andrew said with fake wistfulness and a big grin.

"He's not our little boy anymore," Jack said.

Chad was two years younger than Jack and Andrew and they never tired of reminding him.

"Very funny, guys. Just review the damn raises," Chad said and tossed a stack of papers on Jack's desk.

It only took a minute for Andrew and Jack to review the raises. Chad had been meticulous when it came to his supervisory role of Jennie. He never touched her, never treated her differently than any other employee, and it was no surprise that he had clearly documented the grounds for giving a raise to each of the three employees in question, including Jennie.

"Looks good to me, Chad," Andrew said and Jack echoed his approval.

"You know, Chad, there isn't technically any non-fraternization policy at Sutton. You can date Jennie if you want. I mean, I'm not saying I want you to run out and date just anyone in your division, but we both know Jennie's not just anyone. And, we can file a mutual consent form with human resources for the record. Maybe it's time for you to see where this goes," Jack said.

"Not happening. Next topic." Chad's tone left no room for discussion.

Andrew shrugged at Jack in a silent agreement to drop the topic for now. This had been going on for months and clearly Chad was still hoping his feelings would go away with time.

Andrew would normally have agreed with that plan, but he had to wonder if his feelings for Jill would diminish with time. When she was ready to start dating again now that her divorce was final, would he be okay with watching her date other men?

A big, "Hell, fucking no!" was what came to mind at that

thought. And he didn't think time would do anything to dull that response.

"All right, here's the agenda for the investors from New York. They'll be here for two days and we're packing a lot in with them. Any questions on the packets you got on the agenda for the visit earlier?" Jack asked.

Chad and Andrew glanced through the sheet Jack handed them and both shook their heads.

"Okay, last item," Jack said. "Andrew, there's an administrative assistant in legal who requested a transfer over to financial. Uh..." Jack looked down at his notes. "Theresa Martin. She gets good reports, seems to do her work, but she doesn't have any particular legal training so there's really no reason for us to keep her in legal if she'd rather join finance. Do you have anything open?"

"I might. Jason and Katelyn have been sharing an assistant for a while because neither had a full workload. They're getting to the point where they need more support. I'll double check and get back to you later today," Andrew answered, jotting a note to himself.

He was still busy catching up on everything he'd missed while he was out and was impressed with how much Jason and Katelyn had handled on their own. He might let them keep some of the added responsibilities they'd taken on.

"That's it, then," Jack said, standing.

For the next two days, by the time Andrew pulled himself in late at night, he was exhausted so it made resisting Jill a little easier. He kept telling himself it was better if he didn't go see her. It would make keeping whatever this thing was between them at bay.

By the third day, work had eased up and he couldn't stay away any longer. He missed her.

The last time that had happened was with Blair but he shoved away the reminder. Things with Jill were different. They were friends and friends checked on each other from time to time, didn't they?

He should go make sure her ex hadn't come back around.

Before going to work he cut through the backyards to see if she was awake. As he walked up to the back door of Jill's house, he could see her sipping a cup of coffee and reading something on her laptop at her kitchen island. He tapped on the door and let himself in when she waved in response.

"Hi." Jill greeted him with a genuine smile and he felt himself smile back.

"Hey, stranger. Wanted to see if you felt like getting together tonight." He raised his hands in a gesture of goodwill. "Just as friends. I promise. We sent our investors back to New York this afternoon so I've got nothing going on and I could use a break."

Not that I should be taking that break with you, but I'm a glutton for fucking punishment, apparently.

Jill nodded, but he noticed a wary light in her eye. He would bet she was also thinking through the consequences of the two of them spending more time together.

Jill got up to get a cup of coffee for Andrew and appeared to make a decision.

"Okay. I could use a break, too. I've been knee deep in the website for the past few days and now it's all up to the designers to finish their end of things before we go live."

"Pick you up at seven and we'll go out to dinner?" He took the cup of coffee, using the gesture as an excuse to let his fingers brush along Jill's.

Warm. Just like he knew she'd feel.

He knew taking Jill to a restaurant was too much like a date but staying in seemed too dangerous. At least in public, he couldn't strip her clothes off and use his mouth to see how many times he could make her come.

Fuck.

Needing a distraction, Andrew bent to Rev and rubbed the dog's belly. The curly-haired monkey rolled over and stretched, reveling in the touch and Andrew had to grin as he gave him a few extra scratches.

"Sounds perfect," Jill said.

"Great, I'll see you tonight," he said.

Andrew slipped back out the door and cut back through the yards to Nora's house.

The whole way, he told himself he was playing with fire by seeing Jill this way, but he didn't have the strength to resist.

Jill watched Andrew as he jogged through the backyards to go back to his grandmother's house.

Oh, what a pair of jeans did for that man's ass. It should be a crime to look that good.

She couldn't help but feel a little uneasy, because she already knew they shouldn't get as close as they were. It was one thing to spend time with a group of friends together. Tonight would feel more like a date.

She sighed. She'd just have to keep reminding herself that Andrew was only a friend. And that he could only ever be a friend. Simple in plan, but tough in execution when every second around Andrew was compelling torture.

When he looked at her, she felt flames run through her body. When he brushed her arm or touched her in a casual, friendly way, her body burst to life and a needy ache burned in her core. And so far, Jill couldn't figure out how to stop her response.

She knelt down and threaded her fingers through the curly hair of Rev's side, scratching him as she shared her secret worries with him, in the face of his unconditional love. Dogs were the best.

"I think I may be in over my head, baby. Mommy might get hurt when this is over."

Rev raised his head and looked at her.

She lowered her voice to a whisper to answer his unspoken question. "I think I might really like him. As in 'like him' like him, you know?"

Rev laid his head on his paws and stared up at her with big brown eyes that held no answers for her. She sighed and stood and shook her head at the dog before she crossed the room to the treat cabinet.

"All right, how about a Laughing Puppers Biscuit since you don't seem to have any answers for me, little man?"

Rev jumped up at the name of his favorite treat and offered her a prim and proper sit. Rev was wearing his most innocent look and had straightened himself into his best form to try to win more than one cookie.

The dog knew how to work her.

"You don't fool me," Jill said wryly as she handed him his treat. "I know you're a devil dog." She paused and watched Rev gobble up the treat. "But you like him, too, huh?"

CHAPTER 12

"How does Italian sound?" Andrew asked Jill as they walked to his car.

Jill was appalled to hear her stomach grumble loudly at the mention of Italian food. Andrew turned and threw her a grin.

"Guess that's a 'yes'?"

"Sorry. I forgot lunch and breakfast was pretty small." She blushed. "I tend to get sucked into my work."

She buckled her seatbelt as he steered the car down the drive, pausing at the end before turning onto the road.

"Well, we can fix that. There's a small family-owned place that Nora used to take me to when I was younger. Best gnocchi you've ever tasted. It just melts in your mouth, and the sauce... You'll dream about the sauce for weeks."

Andrew sounded positively wistful as he described the restaurant and Jill knew right away he was talking about Nonna Alda's.

"I haven't been to Nonna Alda's in years!" Her stomach grumbled again. "Oh, the homemade bread. I can't wait for the bread."

He laughed. "Your grandparents took you?"

"At least once every visit. I'm surprised I haven't thought of it since I got back."

Andrew pulled into the parking lot of the small restaurant.

She felt the hot wave of attraction she had come to expect when he placed his hand on the small of her back to walk her into the restaurant. It began at her back, but spread through her whole body, curling her toes.

"Andrew!" A small woman with grey-streaked black hair tied in a braid opened her arms for a hug and kiss. "Joseph, come. Andrew is here."

A very robust man came out of the kitchen and Andrew and Jill were quickly engulfed in hugs and kisses.

The quartet spent a few minutes catching up before Alda showed them to a small booth in a corner. The cozy fireplace near the booth cast a gentle glow on the table.

Jill opened the menu and tried to ignore the lingering feeling she was on a date. She reminded herself repeatedly that Andrew was gregarious and charming with all of his friends. She just needed to ignore the feeling that his attention was all for her. Only for her.

This is not a date. This is not a date. This is not a date. Sigh.

Her chant was having little effect on the date-like atmosphere that hung over their table.

"What are you getting?" she asked him.

"Definitely the gnocchi. Should probably try something else but I can never resist it. What about you?"

"I don't know. I'm torn between the gnocchi and the lasagna. I don't know which one I want more," Jill said and then watched as a grin took over Andrew's handsome face.

"I have a great idea. Get both. I'll get two things, too. That way, I'll be trying something new but still have my gnocchi and you get exactly what you want, too," he announced.

Andrew looked like he was completely serious. Most people would suggest sharing two entrées, but he was suggesting an enormous buffet instead.

"I can't do that!" She shook her head. "I can't eat two meals."

"Why not? Who says you're only allowed to have one entrée? I don't remember there being any rules. We'll get appetizers and two entrées each, *and* we'll get dessert," he said as he waved down their waiter. "We'll just take home whatever we don't eat."

As Jill looked on laughing, he proceeded to order an enormous amount of food and a bottle of Chianti.

"You're crazy." She laughed as she said the words. This man was so different than anyone she'd been with in the past.

It was a dangerous thought. She wasn't with him.

He raised a shoulder in an easy shrug. "So, I'll bring a movie over tomorrow night and we'll gorge on leftovers."

Jill's mind immediately flashed to images of the two of them in her house drinking wine. A great deal of wine. At night. Alone.

Her mouth was suddenly dry and her palms began to sweat. How on earth would she resist the pull of Andrew Weston if they were alone? Resisting him was harder and harder, even tonight, with people around them.

At home, with no one to buffer?

Impossible.

Andrew watched Jill as the waiter delivered their appetizers. He loved that she didn't object too much to his unorthodox dinner order. Most women would balk at eating such a large meal but Jill was being a really good sport about it.

She didn't obsess about her waistline or count calories. She laughed and played along and that appealed to him. Everything about Jill appealed to him.

Andrew did notice the small flash of panic in Jill's eyes when he mentioned coming to her house for dinner the following night. It made him feel triumphant somehow. He'd bet she was as worried as he was about being alone with her. And that thought made him want to be alone with her all the more.

They laughed and talked over a bottle of wine and the

endless buffet of food he had ordered. As he enjoyed her company, he realized resisting Jill might be futile. Her allure might just be more than he could handle.

The thought shocked the hell out of him. He never struggled to compartmentalize the women in his life. When he met a woman, he put her in whatever category she belonged and then he left her there. If she was a friend, she stayed a friend. If she was a fuck-buddy, she stayed that way.

Jill didn't fit in a tidy way into any category. She was wiggling from friend into dangerous, unchartered territory and that was throwing him off. Way off.

The sound of her laughter, the way her hair fell down in waves over her shoulders and onto her breasts, the way she licked her lips when she took a sip of wine. All of the ordinary, everyday things that Jill did were somehow sensual and erotic and sexy as hell.

By the time he walked her to her front door that night, he was hard as a rock and aching to reach for her. He once again had to fist his hands in his pockets just to keep from touching her. He wanted to bury his fingers in the long, soft tendrils of her hair, and lift her face. Capture her lips. Steal just one kiss. Then bury himself deep within her...

Her voice pulled Andrew out of his fantasy.

"Thank you for dinner," she said, lifting up the large bag of leftovers they hadn't finished.

"You're welcome. I had fun," he said, unsure if he should raise the topic of dinner at her house again or just conveniently 'forget.' He knew how it would end if they were alone in a private place.

"Come help me finish them tomorrow night?" she asked and he was torn between relief and regret. Relief that he would be able to spend more time with Jill tomorrow. Regret because he knew he couldn't hold out any longer. If they had dinner alone at her house tomorrow, Andrew would crack. He didn't have any more control where she was concerned.

Say no, asshole.

"Sure." *Oh, fuck. What the hell was that?* "How about seven?" *Stupid, stupid, stupid.*

"Great, see you then," Jill said with a smile and turned and opened her door. Andrew stayed frozen to the spot until she disappeared into the house and shut the door.

CHAPTER 13

The next morning in his office, Andrew was still trying to keep his fantasies about Jill in check. Things were quieter now. The visiting investors were gone and there was a lull in Andrew's projects for the moment.

He wished for more work. Something to keep his mind from drifting back to Jill at every moment because functioning with half a hard on every day, all damn day, was getting old.

Debbie knocked and poked her head into the room.

"Andrew? Got a minute?"

"What's up?"

She came into the room and sat in front of Andrew's desk with her notepad, indicating she had a list of things to go over. He came around his desk and sat next to her.

Debbie was truly his right hand at Sutton, working seamlessly alongside him.

She began going through the items on her list, confirming dates for events, reports that needed to be finalized.

"Oh, and the new assistant from legal transferred in today. I've got her started with Katelyn. Patty is going to show her some of the software she needs to learn, so I think she's all set for now."

"Great, thank you. I'll introduce myself in a bit."

Theresa pasted a smile on her face as she listened to her new boss, Katelyn.

I can't believe I have to put up with this idiot. They should have assigned me to work directly with Andrew.

Theresa had spent the morning figuring out who she needed to compete with to line herself up as Andrew's assistant. From what she'd heard, everyone seemed pretty enamored with Andrew's assistant, Debbie. Theresa couldn't see what the big deal was. The woman wasn't *that* great.

She would work her way into his good graces and show him what she was capable of. She hoped within a few months, she'd be working directly under him.

She smiled at the thought of being *under* him.

We all know what happens with men and their secretaries. Once we're working closely together every day, pulling late nighters and working over lunch, we'll fall in love. That's how these things work.

Theresa might not have been in love before, but she was no idiot. She knew how the world of men and women worked. Knew how men thought and what they wanted. They were easy to manipulate once you got hold of their dicks. Hell, it was what they thought with, wasn't it?

She had to align herself with Andrew and things would fall into place. She hoped things would move faster now that she was in his division. She had worked for six months in legal, hoping Andrew would notice her.

The few times they'd interacted, he smiled at her and she just knew he felt that connection between them, too. But then he would go back to his division and she would be out of sight again. Out of sight, out of mind.

Well, Theresa was damned tired of being out of his sight. She was going to make sure he couldn't forget about her now. The connection they shared was too strong.

"This afternoon, Patty is going to show you how to use the data entry systems we use. Just let her know when you're back from lunch and she'll get you started on the training," Katelyn said.

God... Babble much, lady?

"Sounds great, Katelyn," Theresa said through her fake smile.

"Hey, Katelyn. Hi, Theresa." Andrew offered Theresa his hand. "I think we've met before. Welcome to the team."

There was that zing and the way his eyes met and held hers longer than they should have. It was cute the way he was so professional in front of everyone, but he always found a way to let her know she was special.

He squeezed her hand before letting it go.

"You getting Theresa all settled in?" Andrew asked Katelyn.

"You bet. I'm about to send her to lunch and then she'll be working with Patty for a few days. We probably won't be able to show her everything before the quarterly finance meeting but we'll get her started," Katelyn said.

Theresa turned and beamed at Andrew. "Quarterly meeting? I can help with that." *Perfect opening for me.*

"Oh, don't worry. We're all set. Debbie always has everything set a week in advance and then we just plug in any changes at the last minute." Andrew turned his smile to Katelyn. "These guys run like a well-oiled machine. You can watch things this time. By the time the next quarterly comes around, you'll be able to pitch in."

There was no way she'd wait three months to show Andrew what she could do for him.

"Sure, sounds good. I'll just watch this time." Theresa repeated back his instructions to keep up appearances while she began to run through scenarios.

He probably didn't know how to get her closer to him without it looking odd to everyone else. If he just pulled her right onto his team, issues of seniority would arise. They needed to be more subtle than that.

She'd take care of it for him, though. She'd come up with some way to get herself in that meeting, to get them working more closely together.

"Great. I'm meeting Chad for lunch. Katelyn, do you have everything you need for the conference call with Parker Industries?" Andrew asked as he stepped toward the door.

When Katelyn nodded, he gave a final wave and left the office.

Theresa watched him go. Things would move more quickly now that she had the chance to push them together through work.

She was done waiting for him to make the first move. Modern women were supposed to take charge, weren't they?

CHAPTER 14

*A*ndrew parked in front of Jill's house and rang the bell. He'd thought about cancelling a million times that day, but he hadn't been strong enough to do what would have been best for both of them.

He opened the door and walked in when she called out to come in.

Jill stood in the living room off the front hallway, bent over a tripod and camera that was aimed at the fireplace. The room was lit with several large, professional photography lights complemented by large white umbrella-like things that seemed to angle the light toward the fireplace. Andrew supposed he should have been looking at the photograph over the fireplace but all he could do was focus on Jill.

She was immersed in her work focused only on the camera and whatever magic she saw through the lens. The lights in the room were soft and they bounced off her blond hair and framed her face in a soft glow.

The outline of her slender arms and the breasts he wanted to feast on was clear through the sheer fabric of her shirt. The image sent a blow right to Andrew's gut. It was like he was a teenager again. There wasn't any way to tear his eyes from Jill.

He watched as she made several adjustments to the settings on her camera and then snapped the shutter a half dozen times before looking up at him with a smile.

"Sorry, I'm just trying to get these shots done so I don't have to try to set the lights again tomorrow. When the sunlight comes through the windows in the morning, it will change the way these lights hit the wall and I'll have to start all over again," she explained, gesturing to the wall above the fireplace.

He finally tore his eyes from the woman in front of him and looked at the wall. Above the fireplace hung a gorgeous picture of a dense forest in the fall. The leaves on the trees were an incredible arrangement of golden yellows, burnt oranges, and fiery reds that cast a warm feeling over Andrew as he looked at it.

The glow of the sun shone through the leaves of the trees, creating an effect against the leaves that took the picture from one that merely captured nature to one that was pure art.

"Another one from your fall collection?" he asked, gesturing to the print. The appreciation was clear in his voice.

"Mmm hmm," she said as she flipped through the pictures saved on the disk in the camera to be sure she had the shot she needed.

"It's amazing. All of your work I've seen is so much more artistic than I thought it would be. I thought it would just be pictures of nature, but it's not. You've turned nature into art."

She laughed. "Thanks."

Then he processed what she was doing, taking a picture of one of her pictures. "Uh, why are you taking pictures of your pictures?"

"Remember I said I was starting a website for my work? We're choosing a handful of my pictures to sell as prints and reproductions and this is one of them. I thought I was finished with my side of the website but the site designer decided he wants pictures of the prints as they'll look hanging in someone's home. We could photoshop them into a preexisting photo but this is better. It lets me get the lighting right for each of the images we want to highlight."

She started clearing away the equipment, apparently satisfied with the shots she'd gotten. "We'll also sell things like thank you cards and notepads with the images on them so those all have to be photographed as well. This is the boring commercial side to what I do. Someday, maybe I'll make enough off my pictures to turn this side of things over to an assistant so I can get back to just taking the pictures that I love," she said with a wry smile.

Andrew held up a DVD. "The latest *Bourne* movie. Seen it yet?"

"Nope. Taking a chance I'd like action, huh? What makes you think I didn't want a romantic comedy?" She teased as she started shutting off the bright lights. She seemed to be trying to busy herself with her work and Andrew wondered if she was nervous.

He returned her laugh. "I was hoping it would be okay but I have a sappy romance in the car if we need it, just in case."

"Nice." she smiled and waved him into the kitchen.

Jill pulled out the leftovers from the previous night and began zapping containers in the microwave. They opened the containers and piled plates high – with him taking about three times as much food as she did – before going back to the couch to eat in front of the fireplace.

Jill hit a switch that turned on the gas flames and then curled her feet under her on the couch.

"So," Andrew said between bites of food, "you must travel around a lot to take pictures of different sites. I mean, being a nature photographer, you must have been to some amazing places."

She shook her head as she swallowed a bite of food. "You would think, but I've mostly stayed around here, so far. Jake saw my photography as a 'little hobby' so he never supported trips or anything that would have meant investing time or money in it. Luckily for me, living in Connecticut meant I could drive to the beach and the mountains and take advantage of all four seasons. I do want to start traveling now, though."

Andrew's jaw hit the floor. He couldn't believe anyone could look at Jill's photographs and not see the incredible talent in them. Not want to support that talent, to help it grow. "You're kidding, right?"

She grimaced. "No. Sadly, I'm not. I didn't really see his lack of support as an issue when we were married. I had blinders on to all these faults Jake had. After we separated, it was like coming out of a fog and realizing how one-sided our marriage was. He controlled everything and our whole world was about him."

"Wow. You married an ass," Andrew said bluntly. "Sorry, I guess that's rude, but you really married an ass."

He couldn't stop himself from saying it again. Her ex-husband couldn't be described as anything other than a first-class jackass.

Jill smiled ruefully. "I know. I thought we had this perfect marriage and perfect life but when I look back on it I realize I was fooling myself the whole time. All that mattered to him was his career and how I looked on his arm as his wife. I was an accessory. You know what's sad? He didn't even know how I took my coffee. After seven years of marriage, he didn't even know the most basic information about me like whether I take cream or sugar in my coffee."

Cream. Two sugars.

He couldn't understand how the Jill Walsh he remembered let this happen. Maybe the fifteen-year-old Andrew had put her on a pedestal. Maybe she hadn't been as strong and independent and smart and funny and confident as he thought. She'd let this guy treat her like shit.

"You do realize you're lucky he left you, right?" He finally asked.

Jill winced but then gave him a small smile. "I know. I really do, but it doesn't make me feel like less of a fool. Sometimes I just feel so stupid." She blinked back tears. She looked so vulnerable.

"Oh, Jill, it wasn't your fault." Andrew felt helpless watching her.

"I know. Intellectually, I know it wasn't my fault he cheated, but I can't help feeling like maybe I..." She let the thought drop off, as if not able to voice her fears.

"Ah. That's where the rebound guy comes in." He smiled, bringing them back around to her drunken confession of her rebound plans for him.

Andrew watched as Jill's face flushed and he smiled at her embarrassment. She was really cute when she was bashful. He set his plate down on the coffee table in front of them. He took Jill's empty plate out of her hands and set it down as well.

Andrew turned to face her and placed his hands on her thighs, squeezing just enough to get her attention. He buried a smile when he saw her squirm under his gaze.

He leaned forward and brushed his lips against Jill's cheek. He pulled back and locked eyes with her. Then, slowly, giving her a chance to stop him if she wanted to, he let his mouth graze her delicate jaw line. He dipped his head to her neck and nuzzled her soft skin. Jill gasped and the hitch in breathing matched his own.

Andrew stopped and held his forehead against Jill's, then spoke quietly.

"Then we have a problem. Because I don't think I can watch you rebound with another guy."

She pulled back, her eyes rounded in surprise. The look only lasted a second before she blushed and tried to look away but Andrew placed his hand under her chin and tilted her eyes to his.

"I've tried to resist this, Jill. God knows I've tried, but I just can't. When I'm with you, it takes all I have to keep my hands off you. When I'm not with you, all I'm thinking about is how and when I can get back to you. I want to make you understand how wrong your husband was. I want to be the one to give that to you. To give you back your confidence."

He watched a rush of emotions play across her face. Before

she could answer, he dipped his head to hers and brushed his lips softly over her mouth.

God what he would do to this mouth when she let him free on it. When he had permission to go further.

"Say yes, Jill. Please say yes. Yes to completely no-strings-attached sex for as long as we both want – and to not sleeping with anyone else while we're together." He paused and looked at her as he laid out the terms and watched her turn an even deeper shade of red. "For safety's sake."

He kissed her again, more firmly this time. Gently exploring the full softness of her lips, the sensual curve of her mouth, delving in to touch her tongue with just the very tip of his.

"If either of us wants to end things, we walk away with no ties, no hard feeling, no obligations. Just complete fun, guaranteed to bring back your confidence. And carefully designed for us to remain good friends even after it ends."

He smiled and waggled his eyebrows at her, causing her to break into laughter that diffused the tension.

He was attempting to keep things light, but the few small kisses had pushed his control to the brink. He was hanging on by a thread as he waited for Jill's answer.

"I don't know, Andrew. I know it was my idea, but I've never done anything like that before." She lowered her eyes as if she couldn't look him in the eye. It dawned on him that she might not have been with anyone other than her husband.

He reached out and brushed a finger down her cheek, causing her to look back at him. That single touch shot right to his groin and he knew if she didn't say yes, he needed to get the hell out of there. He'd need to run fast and far in the other direction if she said no. Shit, he should probably run like hell even if she said yes.

"Haven't done what, Jill?"

"Um, just you know, had sex without a real relationship," she said quietly, her eyes big and round.

"Have you been with anyone other than Jake?" He asked her softly.

He knew he probably shouldn't pry into the intimate details of her marriage but he couldn't help himself. He wanted to know what she'd been through. He wanted to fix everything for her. It killed him to think Jill had doubts about herself.

She shook her head and he cursed silently. If Jill had never slept with anyone other than Jake, Andrew would bet she'd had years of that selfish ass satisfying no one but himself in the bedroom.

God, how had she tied herself to such a pig when she could have had any man on the planet drooling over her? She was so smart, and beautiful, so talented. How had she ended up with a guy like Jake?

"Then, you're gonna love this," Andrew said with a grin and leaned in to brush his lips against hers again. He waited a breath to see if she would push him away and when she didn't, he tangled his hands into her hair and pulled her toward him.

Andrew deepened the kiss with a sweep of his tongue.

Jill went stiff for a second but then melted into his hold and he felt her begin to kiss him back.

He broke the kiss and held his forehead to hers as he caught his breath and let her catch her bearings.

"Are you okay with this, Jill?" he asked.

Say yes. Please, say yes.

She nodded and then confirmed with a small 'yes.'

He hadn't realized that he had been holding his breath, waiting to see her answer. He scooped Jill up and carried her upstairs, only mildly aware that as they made their retreat upstairs, Rev cleaned the remnants of food from their plates.

Jill felt a thrill of anticipation ripple over the fear and nerves running through her. Although she had been in one other long relationship before Jake and had been intimate with that man, they had never actually made love.

With her limited experience, Jill was filled with trepidation at the thought that she might not know what to do with Andrew. That she might not be able to satisfy him.

With Jake, their sex life had always been nice, it certainly hadn't been mind-blowing at all. She'd tried hard to please Jake, but when Jill heard some of her friends talk about being with their boyfriends or husbands, she always wondered about their enthusiasm. Her friends made it sound like their experiences were so much better than hers. What if there was something wrong with her?

When she'd thought about a meaningless fling, it seemed like such a great idea. Jill thought she could be as free and laid back about things as some of her girlfriends were in the bedroom. But now, when she was on the verge of actually going through with things, she couldn't help but wonder if this was a monumentally humiliating mistake.

Andrew stopped at the top of the stairs and looked at her expectantly, then laughed when Jill just looked back at him, unsure of what to say.

"Which room, Jill?"

"Oh! Sorry. End of the hall." She gestured to the right. He carried her toward the bedroom she had used as a girl and had taken over again when she returned to her grandparents' house.

Andrew set her down outside the door and then turned the knob and opened the room.

He seemed to sense her hesitation and she marveled at his patience, at the gentleness as he pulled her into another kiss before looking at her.

"I promise. We'll go slowly and you can stop me any time you want to. You say the word and we'll stop, honey."

Jill's stomach fluttered as the endearment fell off Andrew's tongue. Jake had never been very free with things like pet names or affections.

Andrew took her hand and led her to the bed, laying her down but watching her, meeting her gaze. She thought she would drown in his eyes if she weren't careful but she couldn't break the hold he had over her. She really didn't want to break the hold Andrew had over her.

She realized, nervous as she was, she didn't want to pass this up. He already made her feel desirable and wanted again. Something told her that being with him wouldn't be anything like being with Jake. And she was ready for something new, something new and different.

Andrew certainly fit the bill. On all counts.

CHAPTER 15

Andrew lay Jill down on her bed, her golden hair fanning out on the pillow beneath her head – like the rays of sun that shone through the leaves in her photograph.

He marveled at how beautiful she was. From her bright hazel eyes that just grabbed him and held on, to the way her breasts pushed perfectly at the fabric of her shirt as if calling to him.

There wasn't a spot on Jill's body that didn't live up to all of Andrew's teenage fantasies, and then some. All he could think in that moment was that he needed to make this experience perfect for her.

He joined her on the bed, pressing his body over hers. He burned a trail of kisses from the soft spot behind Jill's ear, down her neck, and over the gentle outline of her collarbone. Each kiss sent heat burning right back through his body.

In an instant, Andrew was hard and coiled and barely hanging onto control. He slowly unbuttoned the pearl buttons on her sheer white blouse – the blouse that had been driving him to the brink of insanity the entire night. He slid the light fabric off her perfect, creamy white shoulders.

"God, you're beautiful, Jill." He wasn't surprised to hear his voice was reverent, reflecting his awe. He couldn't honestly say he had ever seen anyone so stunning, so breathtaking as Jill, as she lay before him.

He lowered his head to her breast, taking her nipple into his mouth through the lace of her bra. He sucked and nipped, feeling her body peak under his tongue. And when Jill gasped and pushed her breasts toward him, as if asking for more, he was only too happy to oblige.

He slipped her arms out of her blouse and then turned his attention to her other breast. He used one hand to unfasten her bra and strip it away.

Jill moaned and writhed beneath him with each new spot he found. He always made sure his bed partners were satisfied. He found a certain amount of pride in hearing a woman cry out his name before he allowed himself satisfaction, but pleasuring Jill brought him to whole new heights of arousal himself.

He couldn't get enough of her.

Andrew had to force himself to move slowly, take his time, while he worshipped every inch of her gorgeous body. He ran his hands over the smooth, soft skin of Jill's stomach, over the tiny swell of her tummy, then up to her breasts.

"Tell me if you want me to stop, Jill," he said.

God, please don't ask me to stop. Please.

She let out a gasping sob. "If you stop, I'll die."

Thank you, God.

Andrew laughed softly, his lips against the swell of her breast. He caressed the soft section of skin on the inside of Jill's elbows and wondered if his need to touch her would ever be sated.

He thought he could touch and taste her forever, listening to her soft moans. He watched in awe as Jill responded to his hands. He explored the curves of her legs, her hips, the tiny waist he'd noticed poolside all those years ago.

Andrew moved back up to Jill's mouth and captured her lips again, teasing her lower lip with a small bite. He was rewarded with the press of Jill's body into his.

"Please, Andrew," she begged on a gasp.

"Please, what, sweet Jill? Tell me what you need," he murmured as his hands found their way to the waistband of her pants. He began to slide them down Jill's hips, slowly, torturously.

"More. Touch me more." It was a whispered plea, one he was all too happy to oblige.

With a half groan, half roar, Andrew pulled Jill's legs free of her pants and covered her with his body. He buried his face in her neck, caressing her soft skin with lips that couldn't get their fill as his body met hers. One hand wove into her silken hair and the other dipped between her legs to do her bidding.

Jill was hot and wet and past ready for him. That knowledge sent his own arousal soaring. But Andrew wouldn't give in to the voice in his head that screamed for his own release.

He needed to taste her. He moved down her body, wanting to feel her come on his tongue. To taste the sweet release of her pleasure. To hear her cry out for him.

Using his hands and mouth, he brought her to a crashing orgasm. He drew out Jill's pleasure as long as he could, only stopping when he saw her go completely limp and glassy eyed.

Smiling, Andrew waited for her to come back from the dream state he had induced. He continued to kiss her soft skin, slowly driving himself to the brink.

He knew when he finally entered Jill, he would likely only be able to last seconds before he came and he wanted her fully back with him when that happened.

As Jill began to rouse from the murky ecstasy of the incredible orgasm, she could feel Andrew's mouth traveling the length of her body. He dropped kisses in every erogenous zone she had, most of which she hadn't known existed.

Is this how sex was supposed to be? She had never felt anything close to this kind of passion and heat and sheer pleasure with Jake.

Lying in bed with Andrew, she was suddenly angrier at her ex than she had ever been. Then 'sweet Jill,' the good girl next door, who rarely swore and tried not to hurt anyone's feelings, couldn't help herself.

"That fucking jackass," she said loudly, bringing a rough laugh from Andrew.

"You ain't seen nothin' yet, sweetheart," he promised.

Good Lord. She shivered in response to his words and knew he would follow through on them. Follow through and then some, she would bet.

Andrew quickly donned a condom and slipped in between Jill's legs. He paused while looking into her eyes.

She wrapped her arms around his neck and stared into his eyes. She shivered in anticipation, knowing what was coming would be like nothing she had ever experienced. She strained against him, pressing her hips toward him, silently urging him to enter her.

He smiled and dropped a kiss to her lips.

When he pressed into her in one strong stroke the pleasure brought a cry to her lips. Andrew filled Jill so completely, bringing pure blissful sensation to every ounce of her body, quickly spinning her up and out of control again.

She was drowning in his touch, his kisses, the soft murmuring of his words in her ear. They came together, orgasming quickly, and Jill marveled at the sensations she felt as wave after wave of her orgasm flooded her body.

Andrew collapsed on top of her and the heavy weight of him felt so good. She locked her legs around him, wanting to hold onto every feeling, every sense for as long as she could.

"I can't believe I missed out on that all these years," she said into his chest.

"Mmm hmm." Andrew's answer was muffled by Jill's hair as

he nuzzled his face against her neck. "You truly married the world's biggest ass. The good news is, we have seven years to make up for. We'll have to be diligent and work hard, but I think we can do it."

She laughed as he finally released her and slipped from the bed to clean up. When he returned, she pulled back the covers and he slipped into the bed and pulled her tight to him once again.

She was relieved when he didn't make excuses and run from her right after they'd had sex, though if she were honest, she'd half expected it.

"Well," Jill said with a playful undertone, "I wouldn't want to make you do anything you don't want to do. I mean, you shouldn't have to work so hard to make up for Jake's mistakes."

"I'm very driven," Andrew said. He held her tighter and lightly nipped the soft skin on her shoulder, sending shivers through her again. "And I like a challenge."

Some time later, his teeth scraped the curve in her arm opposite her elbow, a spot she was quickly discovering was directly connected to the hot center between her legs.

She was suddenly ready to get back to work, too.

Jill felt Andrew's erection pressing into her thigh as he quickly brought them both back to life. "I think I like your work ethic, Andrew," she said as he rolled her beneath him for round two of their new project.

CHAPTER 16

*A*ndrew woke to find himself in Jill's bed with Jill wrapped in his arms. He smiled to himself. The feel of her soft body pressed against his felt so right. Like nothing he'd ever felt before. He nuzzled into her soft hair and breathed in her scent, trying to get his fill of her before he had to leave for the day.

Andrew had been in plenty of casual arrangements like the one he and Jill now had. But he never spent the night at the woman's house in any of those arrangements.

He preferred to limit things to sex and hanging out but skip the more intimate portions of the relationship. He didn't snuggle or talk about anything personal. The women he was usually with were friendly, but they never took it past 'hey, how was your day?' That's just how he liked to keep his relationships.

With Jill, Andrew had already broken his rules. Although he wasn't sure why, he really didn't mind that they'd gone beyond those boundaries. In fact, waking up next to Jill was a hell of a lot nicer than he wanted to admit.

Andrew heard the dog whining and realized they hadn't let Rev out last night before they went to bed. It'd be a miracle if they didn't find a puddle somewhere on the floor. He quickly slipped from the bed and threw on his pants. He slipped out the bedroom door and found Rev waiting in the hallway for him.

"Come on, boy," Andrew whispered and they headed downstairs together.

Andrew opened the back door and Rev barreled past him to run outside. He left the back door open so he could keep one eye on the dog while he began the search for coffee. Digging out coffee pods for the single brew machine on the counter, he brewed a cup for himself and one to take up to Jill.

Rev had finished doing his business and was now running around in the woods behind the house chasing deer scents. He put his nose into one of the hollowed-out spots that a deer had burrowed into for the night, sniffed, then ran happily to the next hollow to check that scent.

The deer were long gone, but Rev was having a blast checking out their sleeping quarters. That dog is way too damned easy to please, Andrew thought with a shake of his head.

"Rev, come here," Andrew called. The dog just ignored Andrew and kept running from hollow to hollow. He tried whistling, pleading, yelling, and clapping, but the dog didn't pay any attention.

Andrew heard laughing behind him. He turned to see Jill wearing his t-shirt – which she looked damned good in – as she pulled something out of one of the cabinets.

"Secret weapon," Jill said as she held up a small round cookie. "Laughing Puppers Biscuits. They're Rev's doggy crack."

She went to the door.

"Demon Child!" she called out. Andrew watched as Rev raised his head, sniffed the air and then came racing toward the door at top speed, where he overshot the entrance.

The poor dog tried to skid to a stop but ended up plowing into the cabinets on the other side of the kitchen. Apparently unaffected by the crash, Rev stood, shook his head and pranced daintily back to his mom. He plopped his butt down into a prim and proper looking sit as if he hadn't just flown ass over teakettle through the doorway.

Laughing, Jill delivered the treat and Rev took it over to his bed to eat while she turned her attention to the waiting cups of coffee. Andrew had already doctored both coffees, fixing hers the way she liked it.

"Jill, your dog answers to Demon Child," he commented wryly.

"I know." She grinned. "Isn't he great?"

Shaking his head and laughing, Andrew hooked an arm around her waist and pulled her in for a morning kiss. The feel of her soft and warm from bed had an immediate effect on him.

The kiss turned hot and breathless and needy in a flash and the urge to take her back upstairs quickly overtook Andrew. With a great deal of effort, he broke the kiss before he lost all choice in the matter.

"I have to be at a meeting in half an hour," he said as he watched Jill try to catch her breath. He was relieved to see she was as affected by their kiss as he had been.

"Dinner tonight? Pick you up at seven?"

"Okay," she said.

He knew he was headed for trouble when he felt a huge sense of relief, knowing he'd see her that evening. He kissed her goodbye and walked to the back door, but turned with his hand on the doorknob.

"Hey Jill? Can you wear the dress and boots you wore to Jack's the other day?" he asked.

She gave him a puzzled look. "Sure."

He smiled and walked out the door, sure that he was sinking further and faster into a relationship that he should be running from, but utterly unable to stop.

CHAPTER 17

*J*ill decided to spend the morning in her grandparents' yard taking advantage of nature shots she could get right at home. Jake's lack of support for her career had meant that she learned to take advantage of things she could find close by. She often took trips to the shore or hiked at spots she could reach in a few hours.

Her grandparents' estate actually had some great resources on it. She had some stunning shots of the deer at dusk when they came out to the salt licks she hung on the trees.

This morning she took advantage of the birdbath and feeders she had been keeping full in the front of the house. She succeeded in luring several goldfinches to the feeder by providing the right food and now caught shots of them in the bright morning sun. She was sure the finch shots would make great cards or printed notepads.

Now that she was free of the constraints of her marriage, she really needed to do some traveling. She wanted to capture something bigger than the tiny birds in her front yard. Birds were great for the kind of novelty items that would be sold on her website, but she longed to get back to true art. For that she needed bigger landscapes than her own yard.

When she thought of traveling, she automatically pictured Andrew with her and struggled to push the idea aside. This was not a relationship. If she allowed herself to lose sight of that, she'd be in trouble.

"Jillie Walsh, is that you, dear?" Jill winced a bit when she heard her childhood nickname, but recognized the voice immediately. She turned to see Lydia's welcoming face.

"Hi Lydia! Yes, it's me. Just catching some shots of the finches at the feeders. How is Nora doing? Andrew told me about her hip," she said. She had lowered her camera and walked to the break in the fence between Nora's property and her grandparents' yard.

"She's doing much better. On the mend and ready to get back to her normal routine." Lydia lowered her voice and tilted her head toward Jill. "In fact, she's getting a bit cranky now that she's feeling so much better. The confinement's difficult for her."

Jill nodded. "I imagine that must be hard."

"Will you join us for a cup of tea? Nora saw you out the window over here and wanted to see if you'd like to come for a visit," Lydia said and wrapped her jacket more tightly around her body.

"I'd love to. Let me just put my cameras away and let my dog out for a quick break. Ten minutes?"

"Wonderful. We'll see you then," Lydia said and turned back to Nora's house.

Jill was surprised to feel nervous as she crossed to her front door and went in her house. She walked inside and then out to the backyard to give Rev a potty break.

She'd known Lydia and Nora for years and had been by the house for tea in the past, but when she visited before she hadn't been sleeping with Nora's grandson.

Just thinking about the things Andrew had done to her, with her, for her, brought a flush of heat to Jill's cheeks. She burned with embarrassment at the thought that Nora or Lydia might find out about her and Andrew. She and Andrew may not be teenagers anymore, but she suddenly felt like one.

She called Rev back inside and gave him a cookie, then pulled on her boots again before heading to Nora's house. Lydia answered Jill's knock and Nora called out to Jill from the sitting room off the front entrance.

"Jillie, honey, we're having tea in here." Jill turned into the sitting room with Lydia following behind her.

"Nora, I was so sorry to hear about your hip." Jill meant every word of her greeting. She had always liked Nora.

Nora didn't act anything like a grandmother and had always been fun. Nora and Lydia had been genuinely interested in Jill when she visited over the years.

"Oh, pish!" Nora waved a hand through the air dismissively. "It's fine. I'm almost back to normal now. I'll be out and about in no time, thanks to that brute of a physical therapist who comes to torture me four times a week. Andrew hired him to torment me."

Jill felt herself blush at the mention of Andrew. Trying to calm her nerves, she sat in a wingback chair while Lydia poured tea and offered Jill a cookie.

"Now then," Nora said, "tell me what's going on with you and my grandson."

Jill barely managed to choke down the sip of tea that was in her mouth without spitting it out from pure shock. Why she would be shocked that Nora would be so blunt, escaped Jill at the moment. The woman never was one to beat around the bush.

"Uh, well..." she struggled for words to respond. Lydia settled herself in next to Nora, looking like she was getting ready for a good tale.

"Please, dear. I know he's graduated from watching you through the windows to crossing the backyard and driving his car up and down your driveway several times this week. I assume Andrew's grown up enough that he hasn't begun peeping in your windows or anything like that. So, fill me in. What are your intentions with my grandson?"

"My intentions? I, uh, well." Jill paused, racking her brain for a response. "We're just spending time together. Yes, spending time together," she explained as firmly as she could.

"Oh, bother. I had rather hoped it was more serious than that. He needs someone to help him forget what that witch of a fiancée did to him. I thought maybe you'd finally be the one to help him get past that. He's always loved you, after all." So much of what Nora said left Jill stunned. She didn't know which part of that statement was more confusing.

Fiancée? Always loved Jill?

"Oh, um, it's not really like that. I'm not really ready for any kind of serious relationship after my husband, well, after that whole debacle." Jill felt the blood rush to her face yet again and wondered if Nora realized Jill was sleeping with Andrew.

"Well, don't worry. My grandson's got a reputation for being good in the sack, so he'll help you forget that damn fool you married," Nora said matter-of-factly. Lydia looked on and nodded in agreement over the rim of her cup of tea while Jill's face flamed hot and red.

"Oh!" *Well, so much for wondering.* Jill sat in stunned silence for a few moments, not at all sure what to say to that, but Nora and Lydia had apparently moved on to other topics.

They began to pepper her with questions about her photography, whether her grandparents might return for the summer, her dog – and when Rev could come by for a visit. By the time Jill left an hour later, they had covered every topic imaginable.

Unfortunately, all Jill could think about was the fact that Andrew had once had a fiancée he hadn't mentioned, that he'd supposedly loved Jill for years and that his grandmother knew she and Andrew were shacking up.

∽

Andrew wasn't sure what had come over him where Jill was concerned. He'd told her he would pick her up for dinner, but for some unknown reason, he decided to cook for her.

That afternoon, he found himself at the grocery store, picking up fixings for the only meal he knew how to make: chicken and pasta with French bread. He grabbed a couple bottles of wine and a pie for dessert.

As he drove to Jill's, he tried to figure out just what the hell was going on. How had this woman gotten under his skin so damn far and so damn fast? Why the hell didn't he have any desire to try to shake her?

At first he thought things were different with her because she was the only woman he had ever hooked up with that was also a part of his circle of friends. Or maybe it was the fact he and Jill had known each other for so many years. Or that they spent time together as friends before being intimate.

He exited the highway and began the series of turns that would bring him to the side-by-side estates where he and Jill lived. All day, he'd thought about last night.

Yes. There'd been thoughts of holding her, touching her, tasting her that grabbed him. But, he also wanted to talk to Jill, laugh with her, see her damn dog. He wanted to tell her that he had some ideas for places they could travel to for her photography.

Oh, shit. Was he really making plans for them to travel together?

He needed to figure out how to stop this. To slow shit down before things went too far. He knew the only way to stop the escalation of this relationship was to stay away from Jill altogether, because as long as he was around her, he couldn't stop the feelings, no matter how hard he tried.

Who the hell was he kidding? He couldn't stay away from her at this point. There was no fighting the pull he felt toward Jill, no trying to ward off what was happening. Andrew knew at that moment, he needed to be around Jill like he needed air to breathe.

CHAPTER 18

*J*ill sipped the glass of wine Andrew had poured her and watched as he simmered sauce and stirred pasta into boiling water. If anyone had asked Jill an hour ago if there was any way an apron could make Andrew Weston look sexy, she'd have thought they were nuts.

But damn, what an apron did for that man. Everything Andrew did was sexy though. It shouldn't have come as a shock that cooking would look so good on him.

Jill had just finished telling him that Nora and Lydia had invited her to tea that morning.

"Uh, oh. Did Nora have anything to say about us?" Andrew asked as he slathered garlic butter on the French bread and popped it into the oven to toast.

"Oh, you bet she did. What I don't get is how she knows about us? I was hoping she didn't have a clue!" Jill said.

"Oh, that woman knows more than a voodoo priestess gifted with the sight. Nothing gets past Nora and if it does, Lydia is there to pick up the slack," he answered over his shoulder.

Stirring the pasta sent the muscles on his broad shoulders and taut back into motion, mesmerizing Jill. She remembered grabbing those muscles as Andrew drove into her over and over and suddenly she was more than just distracted. She was hot and flustered.

Thankfully, the thought of her conversation with Nora and Lydia quickly brought her back down to earth.

"Well, she knows about us. Nora was rather blunt about us. Wanted to know if I was helping you get over your fiancée."

Jill saw the sliver of a moment when Andrew froze at the mention of his former fiancée. His hesitation was so brief, it was barely noticeable but she had been watching for a reaction, wondering if it would be there.

She wouldn't ask him to explain about his fiancée or ask what happened, but she wanted him to know that she knew. She waited quietly, to see if he would say anything. She was beginning to think Andrew was going to pretend that she had never said the 'f' word when he finally spoke up.

"She told you about that, huh?" he asked. He plated up their dinners and joined Jill on a stool at the center island to eat.

She decided to gloss over the fiancée, redirecting the conversation to give Andrew an out if he wanted it.

"Nora asked me what my intentions toward you were. When I told her we were just spending time together, she told me you have a reputation for being – and I swear to you, I'm quoting here: 'good in the sack.' It was by far the most uncomfortable conversation I've ever had," Jill said.

Andrew's fork hung in midair as he stared, open mouthed at Jill, a horrified expression on his face. "She did not. Please tell me she did not say that to you. Of course she did. Who am I kidding? This is Nora we're talking about."

Jill just laughed as she watched Andrew try to process her conversation with Nora.

"At least you didn't have to sit there and figure out how to explain our relationship to her," she said.

Andrew grinned at that. "'Spending time together,' huh?"

"I couldn't think of any other way to tell her I was banging her grandson." Jill blushed furiously as the frank colloquialism left her mouth.

She picked up her wine glass and sipped to try to cover her embarrassment, but Andrew leaned in, moved the wineglass out of his way and kissed her soundly on the cheek.

"I like banging you, Jillie Walsh."

As they finished their dinner, Andrew felt his body go from relaxed with laughter to intense with heat. And that heat was directed at Jill. It amazed him that she could affect him so strongly. With a look, she could twist his body into a tight, tense coil ready to explode. Needing release.

He put down his wine glass and reached his hand across the table toward her. She placed hers in his and let Andrew draw her up and around the table. He pulled her down onto his lap and buried his head in her neck, breathing in her scent as arousal filled every cell of his body.

This was quickly becoming his favorite place to be.

"Watching you in these boots at Jack's house was pure torture," he whispered to Jill. His voice was throaty and hoarse with desire.

When Andrew's mouth met Jill's she kissed him back with her whole body. She pressed herself close to him, as if willing him to take her upstairs.

He responded quickly to her silent demands, to her quiet plea with her body. In one smooth movement, he lifted Jill and carried her up to her bedroom. He lay her on the bed and took off his clothes.

As Andrew pulled off his shirt and unbuttoned his pants, Jill watched him, making no move to remove her own clothes.

He needed her naked, now.

"Sweater. Off." Andrew ordered Jill to remove her clothes

with the patience and sophistication of a caveman, bringing a smile to Jill's lips. He couldn't muster any more control right now. The way she responded to him, the way she pressed her body into him sent him to the edge of control so quickly, he couldn't breathe.

She pulled the sweater dress up over her head and exposed her incredible body. She wore matching white lace bra and panties and the sight of her in pristine white – virginal white – almost sent Andrew over the top.

He groaned as Jill reached behind her back and unhooked her bra, slipping it off her shoulders and letting it drop to the bed beside her.

She reached for her cowboy boots but he had other ideas.

"Those stay on. Get rid of the panties, Jill."

He saw her swallow and hesitate, but she never moved her eyes from his.

"Now, Jill," he said quietly. He was hanging onto his control by a thread.

He froze as he watched her slip the small scrap of white lace down her hips, over those heavenly thighs. She pulled her panties down over the sexiest fucking cowboy boots Andrew had ever seen.

Jill lay back down on the bed and Andrew swallowed a curse as he crawled up the bed to her, predatory in his need for this woman.

He couldn't taste enough of Jill. His hands could never hold enough of her and his erection all but screamed her name as it strained toward her body.

"I can't wait, sweetheart. I'll make it up to you, I promise, but I can't wait."

Her laughter answered him as he slipped on a condom but she quickly lost her laughter and her breath when he buried himself in her in one swift, powerful stroke. Jill's arms and legs, complete with cowboy boots, came around his hips just as he'd pictured them. He heard her breathe his name in his ear and any scrap of control that was left was torn away.

He brought them both to release faster than he'd ever imagined possible. In tandem.

He lay on top of Jill, desperate to catch his breath and regain the balance that she'd taken from him. Taking her with him, he rolled to the side and they lay tangled together as they both fought to recover.

"I'm sorry." Andrew grinned at Jill. "From the moment I saw those boots on you, all I could think about was having my hands on you again, tasting you, feeling your muscles around me, your nails clawing at my back. I thought I'd go mad waiting. Give me ten minutes and I'll make this up to you." He closed his eyes as he finished his rushed apology.

"I'm not complaining. That was perfect. You sure have a way of bringing back a woman's confidence."

Her breath was still coming faster than usual and she ran her hands over his chest. She moved them over his arms in a greedy gesture that showed Andrew she'd be ready for more just as soon as he was.

He grinned in response. "I aim to please. After all, confidence is what this is all about, right? Well, that and showing you things Jackass never did." He had given up using her ex-husband's name and now referred to him solely as 'Jackass' or 'the Ass.'

"I think I'm a little in love with those boots," he said as he caught his breath.

Jill laughed. "I have a little bit of an addiction to boots and handbags. There are probably nine or ten pairs of boots for us to work our way through and I'm always willing to buy more when we run out."

Andrew's answer was a low groan as he began to kiss her neck again, exploring the soft curves and eliciting tiny moans of pleasure from Jill.

"I'll give you my credit card. Buy as many as you want." He talked as his mouth roamed her body.

Her heated hands soon had his body springing back to life and they made love again, with Andrew worshiping her body slowly, but no less hungrily this time.

He took his time bringing her to orgasm, first with his hands, then his mouth, before finally entering her. He brought her to a final lazy, long orgasm that he joined her in before they collapsed in a tangled mess in the middle of Jill's large bed.

CHAPTER 19

*A*s they lay wrapped in one another's arms with nothing between them but the occasional tangle of sheets from the bed, Andrew found himself wanting to explain about Blair. He had never told another woman about Blair and never thought he could bring himself to tell the story, to repeat what she and his parents had done.

As with everything with Jill, things he thought he could never do simply happened.

"Her name was Blair." Andrew felt Jill's breath catch and he knew that she understood immediately who he was talking about. He felt her hand run up and down his back in slow, steady strokes but she made no move to pressure him for the story or try to lure details out of him.

"We met when I was at Yale Business School. She worked on campus at one of the coffee stands. She was so beautiful and she had me convinced that I was in love, that we were in love, before I knew what hit me.

"Somehow, I never saw her for what she really was. She was conniving and manipulative, but I didn't see any of that until it was too late. Later I learned Blair had me targeted from the beginning, knew my family had money." Andrew let out a rough burst of laughter but there was no humor in it.

Jill didn't answer, but her hand kept up the steady support on his back. The calm patience he needed as memories of a pain he knew he'd never fully recover from washed over him.

"We were attracted to each other from day one. I liked the joking and flirting every morning when I picked up my coffee, but it was all a setup. She told me she was on the pill, but I found out later that was a lie. In the beginning we used condoms anyway but as soon as I told her I loved her, she told me we shouldn't use them anymore because we were in love and would only be with each other.

"I can't believe what an idiot I was. I was in graduate school for God's sake. It's not like I was in high school, or even college. I was an adult. I should have been able to read her better. To see the lies for what they truly were." Andrew was surprised at how dead and flat his voice sounded as he talked about Blair.

"As soon as Blair got pregnant, she went to my parents. She never even told me she was pregnant. My parents told me two days later that they had 'fixed my problem' for me. They paid her $500,000 to abort the baby and leave town. They knew I would want to marry her if she was going to have my child and they never considered Blair to be good enough to be a Weston. Blair never wanted a child. She wanted leverage."

Andrew didn't tell Jill about the nightmares. He didn't have them very often anymore but for a long time after Blair's abortion, he woke in a cold sweat. He remembered flashes of the dream, his baby crying as he ran from room to room looking for it but he could never find it. He didn't even know if the baby was a boy or a girl.

"I was a wreck for a week. Jack and Chad came and managed to get me out of my drunken stupor and brought me here to Nora's. Nora and I both cut all ties with them. We haven't had any contact since then."

Andrew finally chanced a glance at Jill's face and saw tears.

"Don't cry sweetheart, don't." He wiped the tears from her cheeks as he held her in his arms.

Andrew had always believed what happened with Blair was only partially his fault, but on some level, he supposed he always felt like a fool for letting Blair string him along that way. For not seeing how manipulative and cold she really was.

Now, as he told Jill about her, he didn't feel that way at all. For the first time since news of the abortion, he felt free of it. Free of the guilt.

He would always feel the pain of losing his child and not knowing what could've been, what it would have felt like to hold his baby. To raise his son or daughter. But lying there with Jill, Andrew felt as whole and complete as he ever had.

Jill ran her hands through Andrew's hair, trying to soothe, to stop the pain. As she listened to his story, she couldn't imagine the betrayal, the anger and hatred, the sadness he must have felt when he found out what Blair and his parents had done behind his back.

He'd lost it all. The woman he thought he loved, his child, and his parents.

Jill's problems with her marriage and her emotional state after her divorce seemed pale in comparison to what this incredible man had been through.

She was amazed that Andrew still had so much love in him, despite what had happened. She'd seen the love he gave to his friends, the bond he had with Nora. She knew how fun and happy he could be, how much he made her laugh and how much he cared about what she was feeling, and she loved that he still had that in him despite what he'd been through.

Jill and Jake had never had children but Jill had miscarried once. The pain of the loss she felt had threatened to swallow her for a long time after. She could only imagine what Andrew's loss was like. To find out about the baby after it was too late, must have torn him apart.

She cupped Andrew's cheeks and placed a soft, tender kiss on his lips. A kiss that Jill hoped spoke to him of all that she was feeling but couldn't say to him. She wanted to be able to wash away his pain.

She threaded her fingers in his hair and trailed slow, sensuous kisses across his cheek and down the strong line of his jaw. She kissed his neck, feeling the scratch of stubble against her skin. She stopped to brush her lips across his neck, tickling and teasing.

"Jill," Andrew breathed. There was a note of pleading in his voice and suddenly the air was no longer filled with pain and sympathy. She was no longer trying to ease his hurt or make up for past cruelties. Even with all that Andrew left unspoken – when he said her name, he turned the air to heat and passion.

His hands came around her waist and he lifted her up to straddle his hips. She pressed down, feeling the hard length of him tease her as she continued her exploration of his body. Every kiss she laid on him sent shivers back through her. She reveled in the feeling of Andrew's hard muscles under her lips.

She stopped to tease his nipples with her tongue and then continued down to the hard plates of his stomach, the taut plane that led to his groin. She nipped at his skin, and listened as Andrew's breath hitched beneath her. With each kiss, each lick, every teasing lick, she hoped he was forgetting all about Blair's betrayal. Of the memories she'd raised.

In the blink of an eye, her play was interrupted as Andrew rolled them, hoisted her under him and came down over her body with a growl that told her he didn't have the patience for anything more. He reached in the bedside stand and rolled on a condom before entering her quickly and burying himself to the hilt.

"God, what you do to me," he groaned. He lay still for a moment letting them both catch their breath.

She laughed, but it was thready and needy. "I know the feeling."

He moved languidly inside her, rocking his hips into her again and again as he stared into her eyes. Slowly, teasing, Andrew drew himself out of Jill and then deliberately plunged to the hilt again. Her eyes closed but he whispered to her to open them.

"I want to see those gorgeous eyes. I want you to be looking into my eyes when I make you come," he said as he drove into Jill again and again. Within minutes she was calling his name just as he was crying out to her.

She wrapped her arms and legs around him and held him afterwards. She trailed her hands over his back and marveled at the feel of his strong, hard body in her arms. They stayed that way for a long time before rolling to the side and drifting off to sleep and she knew she was dangerously close to losing her heart to this man.

CHAPTER 20

Andrew woke some time later and slipped from the bed to use the bathroom. When he came back into the room, he spotted Rev at the foot of the bed. Something seemed off. The dog was lifting his feet in a funny way and almost looked as if he couldn't get his legs to work properly.

Andrew shook Jill awake gently and whispered in her ear. "Honey, I think something's wrong with Rev. He's acting funny."

Jill was up and out of the bed in a flash, and on the floor with Rev.

"Shhh, lay down Rev," she cooed to the dog as she coaxed him to lie down on his side. Rev's legs stuck straight out in front of him, quivering and tense. His eyes looked glazed and he didn't fight Jill as she cradled him.

"What's wrong with him?" Andrew asked over her shoulder as he watched her comfort Rev.

"He has seizures sometimes. It's not a big deal. He'll be like this for a few minutes and then he just snaps out of it and it's over. He might be a little tired after, but that's it."

"Can they give him medicine for them?" He sat on the floor behind Jill and wrapped his legs and arms around her and the dog. Even though she was calm and trying to act casual, he could tell she was worried.

"They can, but they won't do that until he starts to have them more frequently. The meds have some serious side effects, so his vet will only start him on them if his seizures happen more than once a month. As long as they aren't that often and they stop within five minutes, we don't need to do anything other than make him comfortable and safe when they're happening."

She looked down at Rev as she talked and petted gently until his legs began to relax.

"See? He's coming out of it already," she said and smiled up at Andrew.

He felt like he had been punched in the gut when she smiled at him like that.

Somehow, someway, in the short span of just a few days, this woman had reached deep down into his soul, touching a part of him that he had buried the day he found out what Blair had done.

Andrew wasn't sure he wanted anyone reaching that deep inside him but neither did he want to fight his response to Jill.

He helped her lift Rev up onto the bed with them and they fell asleep with the dog between them. Just before slipping into sleep Andrew wondered how the hell he ended up snuggling with a giant, curly mop of dog hair instead of Jill, but was surprised to realize he didn't care.

Shit.

CHAPTER 21

*A*fter leaving Jill's house the following morning, Andrew pulled into Nora's driveway and let himself in through the front door.

"Nora, Lydia!" he called out as he walked back toward the kitchen. He found the ladies sitting in the breakfast nook together, looking up at him as innocent as can be. Andrew had learned a long time ago that these two were anything but innocent.

"Good morning, dear," Nora greeted him. "Will you join us for breakfast?"

He leaned his large frame in the doorway, crossing one foot over the other. Arms crossed, he leveled a hard stare at both women.

"Is that a 'no'?" Nora asked.

"You told Jill about Blair." He knew his stance and tone would have gotten results in the boardroom, but Nora refused to budge.

Lydia squirmed a bit and got up to fidget with a plate of eggs and toast for Andrew, but a little fidgeting didn't appease him.

"Sit, eat. You'll feel better." Lydia passed Andrew the plate and tried to herd him to the table.

He held his position for a moment, but then gave in to Lydia and sat down. He couldn't resist the two women when they ganged up on him and remaining angry was just too hard in the face of Lydia's cooking.

The three sat and ate while Lydia and Nora chatted about mundane affairs: the weather, their plans to have the upstairs library painted, a charity event they'd be hosting in a few months. Andrew finished his meal and brought the conversation back around to Jill and Blair.

"Nora, you told her about Blair," he said more emphatically.

"I must have had a moment. I forget who knows about Blair and who doesn't." She tried her best to look innocent but Andrew knew better than that.

"You're more lucid on a bad day than I am on my good days, so don't give me that crap. You know perfectly well that outside of this family, Chad and Jack are the only people who know about Blair."

He didn't need to explain that his reference to family encompassed Lydia.

His grandmother raised her chin. "Then maybe it's high time to change that. If you don't talk about things like that, you can't possibly have a future together."

"Nora," he said with patience but still an undertone of firm resolve, "Jill and I aren't going to have a future. We're just having fun together. Nothing serious."

As he said the words, he knew they weren't true. A week ago, hell, even a day ago, they might have been true, but they weren't anymore. He felt more for Jill than he had ever felt for another woman.

Shaking off his thoughts, he stood and carried his plate to the sink. He rinsed it and put it in the dishwasher then turned to the women.

"I have to get to work, but really, Grandmother, stay out of this. I don't need you interfering with Jill and me." He hoped his use of the word grandmother would help to convey the seriousness of his message.

Andrew never called Nora anything other than Nora, but the effect was lost. She sat looking as unflappable as ever.

"Yes, dear. Have a nice day at work," Nora said.

Those two were incorrigible. Andrew rolled his eyes, kissed Nora and Lydia on the cheek and walked back out to his car.

Debbie and Andrew leaned over the stacks of papers in front of them, checking to be sure everything was in place for the quarterly finance meeting the following day. Jennie stood next to them, ready to help if they needed any last-minute items. Although Jennie was usually out on assignment working with companies that hoped to gain the financial backing of Sutton Capital, when she was between outside jobs, she floated the office, helping out with secretarial support as needed.

The quarterly meeting would include all the board members of Sutton Capital and a handful of the larger investors. Although there was always a flurry of activity leading up to it, by now, the groups had the process down to a science.

"Let's add a printout of the estimated costs of the Haynes Project, just in case we have time to discuss that. If not, we'll push that to the next quarter," Andrew said. "Other than that, everything looks great. I think we're ready."

"Perfect," Debbie said. "I'll set out everything in the conference room tonight and lock it. We'll be ready to go in the morning. I'm planning to be here a couple hours early."

He knew she'd be there by six o'clock the next morning. She and Andrew were always the first in on a quarterly meeting day, both of them arriving early and not leaving until late evening. Andrew looked at his iPhone.

"I've got a meeting with Chad and Jack in a few minutes but then I'll be free for the afternoon if anything comes up," he said.

∽

"I'll print the Haynes estimates," Jennie said and took off toward her desk down the hallway.

She quickly printed out the report and then went to the photocopy room to make enough copies for everyone attending. She would make two extra copies in case they were needed.

When she got there, Theresa was counting stacks of papers. Jennie had known Theresa before she came to the finance division, and for some reason, the woman always rubbed Jennie the wrong way.

It was odd, actually. Jennie usually got along well with everyone. It was one of the reasons she was good at her job. She was able to go into a wide variety of companies and make friends quickly and easily during her time there.

Theresa struck Jennie as insincere somehow. There wasn't any one thing she could put her finger on. But for some reason, she always felt uneasy around Theresa.

"All done with the copier, Theresa?" she asked.

"Yup. All yours," the other woman said. "What are you working on?"

"Oh, just getting some things ready for the quarterly," Jennie replied lightly and was surprised to see Theresa scowl.

"I thought everything was finished for that." There was a bitter tone to her statement and Jennie fought the urge to roll her eyes. She'd seen this kind of weird competitiveness at some of the other companies she'd worked in but it wasn't something that happened a lot at Sutton.

It was something fostered in the environment there. They all pitched in and helped out. If something needed to get done, you did it.

"Oh, this is just a last-minute report."

"I told Andrew I was available if there was anything he needed. He should have asked me," Theresa said. Her tone was off. Cold.

Jennie offered a shrug, not sure how to respond to Theresa's odd comment and behavior. She decided to make light of the situation and brushed off the woman's discontent because Andrew asked her for help instead of Theresa.

"Oh, well. He probably forgot. Andrew's head has been all up in the clouds lately. He's got a new girlfriend so he's in lala land a lot of the time right now. You know, excitement of a new relationship and all," Jennie said.

Shit. She shouldn't be talking about his personal business at work, but the woman had her flustered. Not to mention, Jennie knew the contrived excuse wasn't true. Even though Andrew was happier than Jennie had ever seen him since he started dating Jill, she had never seen him drop the ball at work.

He was just as focused and on top of things as ever, but Jennie was grasping at straws to try to diffuse Theresa's absurd anger. She thought if she could explain away Andrew's actions, it would calm the angry attitude.

Boy was she wrong. Theresa stiffened, pressed her lips together in a line so they all but disappeared on her face, and waltzed out of the room without a word.

Wow. Scary.

Jennie turned back to her copies, relieved at least that Theresa had gone away. If the woman kept that kind of attitude up, she would find herself losing more and more assignments.

Theresa focused on breathing as she walked back to her desk. Her hands clutched the stack of copies too tightly, creasing the once neat pages.

Girlfriend? Shit. This can't be happening.

She needed to get herself lined up to work with Andrew so he could see how well they would work together. His interest in her had been clear in their previous encounters, but she knew there was the potential for so much more between them.

If they worked together closely, he'd be able to see the chemistry they had. He would see that he and Theresa could be so much better than whatever whore he was dating. She clenched her fists.

Fucking whore. Trashy, slutty, fucking whore, putting her hands all over what's mine. Andrew is mine.

Theresa folded her hands in her lap and sat quietly at her desk slowly breathing in through her nose and out through her mouth. Her therapist had taught her the technique and she'd gotten good at using it when she needed to keep calm.

Now was the time to stay calm. She would just bide her time and work on getting closer to Andrew so he could see what they had between them was different. Special. So much more than anything he could have with someone else.

CHAPTER 22

Andrew lay with Jill in his arms listening to the soft sounds of her breathing. They shared a quiet evening at her house, snuggling on the couch and watching a movie – romantic comedy this time. They'd gone to bed early and two orgasms for Jill and one incredible orgasm for Andrew later, she had fallen asleep in his arms.

His appreciation of the sweet sounds of Jill while she slept was disrupted with the shrill sound that indicated an incoming call from Debbie. He shifted Jill over to free his arm and reached for his phone on the nightstand.

"Debbie? What's up?" It wasn't unheard of for his assistant to call him late at night and with the quarterly meeting the following day, it was possible that she had remembered some small detail they'd forgotten that day.

"Andrew, it's Bob," Andrew heard Debbie's husband say on the other end of the phone.

He felt a chill at the sound of Bob's voice and knew right away something was wrong.

"What's wrong, Bob. Is Debbie okay?" he asked. He felt Jill sit up next to him.

"Debbie's in the hospital, Andrew. She was attacked tonight outside our apartment," Bob said.

Andrew heard the words catch in the other man's throat.

"Attacked? When? Where?" He leapt from the bed and started to dress.

"It looks like a mugger. Debbie didn't see anything other than someone in a dark ski mask and dark clothes. They came up behind her in the stairwell and stabbed her in the back, then grabbed her purse and ran. She's okay. Just a flesh wound, really. She's frightened and shaky but not hurt badly," Bob said.

"Thank God." Andrew sank back down onto the bed, the adrenaline that coursed through his veins making him shaky. "Can I do anything? Do you need me at the hospital?"

"No. They'll release her tonight. She was able to walk the rest of the way to the apartment to get me. She's really not hurt badly. The police thought the mugger must be new at this because it was such a shallow cut. They said it showed hesitation. Debbie wanted me to tell you she won't be in the office tomorrow but she's worried because of the quarterly meeting."

"She doesn't need to worry. She has everything ready to go. We'll be fine. Tell her to rest and take as much time as she needs. I'll check on her tomorrow."

"Thanks, Andrew. I appreciate that."

"Hey. Bob. Uh, I don't mean to pry but I thought your apartment was in a pretty safe complex. Do you guys need help finding somewhere else to stay?" Andrew thought of Debbie as a lot more than an assistant and the idea that she lived somewhere dangerous made him uneasy enough to broach the subject, uncomfortable as it might be.

"That's the weird thing. We live in a very safe neighborhood. There haven't been any other reports of muggings. The lights in that section of the stairwell had been broken and the police thought it was likely done by the mugger. I don't know what to think now, Andrew." Bob sounded frustrated.

"Well, if any other incidents happen there let me know and we'll help you guys find something else quickly. Tell Debbie not to worry about work. I'll swing by and see her after the meeting tomorrow, if it's not too late."

He hung up the phone and turned to find Jill watching him. She seemed to have guessed most of what had happened from the side of the conversation she'd heard.

"Debbie was mugged? She must have been so scared!"

Jill hadn't met Debbie yet but Andrew had told Jill about her.

"She's okay. Just a few stitches. She's scared, though. Someone came up behind her in the stairwell and stabbed her and grabbed her purse ... It was only a flesh wound, but it's scary to think what could've happened."

He pulled Jill onto his lap and buried his face in her neck.

"Your heart is racing a mile a minute," she said, her hand on his chest.

He didn't answer. He couldn't. He was too busy thinking about what he would have done if Jill had been the one hurt. He pulled her tighter and held on until his pulse stopped racing.

He began to nuzzle Jill's neck, brushing his lips against her soft skin. Buried in the warmth of her neck was turning out to be one of Andrew's favorite places to be. He could immerse himself forever in Jill, breathing in her scent. Somehow, in the middle of winter, she smelled like summertime. Like grass and sun and sand. Like happiness. And contentment.

He felt her squirm beneath him and he laughed. "I guess we're awake now."

"You certainly are," she laughed and he felt her wiggle her bottom on his lap, where he was already hard and ready for her.

He gripped her hips and held her tighter. Jill dropped her mouth to his and Andrew captured her lips. Hot and soft and all his. Only his.

He ran his hands up her body and watched her respond to his touch. His palms grazed the sides of her breasts and she leaned further into them, her hands playing through his hair. Andrew groaned and gathered Jill, flipping her over onto the bed. He came down over her, pressing his thigh between her legs, spreading her legs for him.

She sighed and lifted her body toward his. She deepened their kiss and Andrew let his hands roam her body, exploring and teasing. They moved slowly, taking their time. He knew then that he would never need anyone else to satisfy him.

Only Jill. He could never tire of her body. The soft moans and sighs she made. The urgent movements when she needed more of him.

"Andrew," Jill gasped. He would never tire of the sound of his name on her lips. He stroked Jill's core, teasing with just the amount of pressure that always seemed to bring her to the edge. He watched her beautiful face, watched her come apart in his arms and knew he would never tire of that, either.

Jill's body was still reeling when Andrew slid back between her legs. He kissed her lips...deep, sensual kisses that kept her head up in the clouds. She felt like she could get drunk on his kisses. His touch. The taste of him. He quickly found a condom in the bedside drawer and rolled it over his hard, thick length.

She felt him between her legs, pressing into her, deeper than anything she'd felt before. Jill moaned and pulled him closer, wanting more of him. Wanting all she could have.

"I can't get enough of this feeling," she whispered.

He groaned. A deep rumbling sound Jill felt deep in his chest.

"I could wrap my arms and legs around you and hang on forever," she said, and Andrew's groan came again while he drove deeper and harder.

"You're killing me, Jill," he said as he crushed her mouth with his and swallowed her small gasps and moans.

She raised her hips, pushing him deeper. She made small circles with her hips, meeting each stroke of his with a circling stroke of her own. She felt his breathing become uneven, raspy. She felt an erotic power as his body coiled for release above her.

With a deep roar, Andrew's resolve broke and Jill's orgasm began with his. He continued to drive into her, drawing her orgasm out long after his own ended. Jill fell, exhausted, beneath him.

CHAPTER 23

Andrew called Jack on the way to the office and filled him in on Debbie's attack. He had already called Patty earlier that morning to let her know she needed to cover for Debbie that day. At Sutton, they always had backup plans in place. And backup plans for the backup places.

When Andrew pulled into the parking garage at the office, Patty was just stepping out of her car.

"Have you heard anything more from Bob? Is Debbie back at home?" She asked as they walked toward the elevator together.

"No. I didn't want to call too early today. We'll send some flowers over to her this morning and then take a break from the meeting to call her a little later," he said.

When they stepped out of the elevator into the lobby of Sutton Capital, Andrew was surprised to see Theresa was already there. He and Debbie were usually the only ones to arrive at six o'clock unless, like today, Patty came in. The rest of the team would arrive in an hour or so.

"Good morning, Theresa," Andrew said. "What are you doing here so early?"

"Oh, I just thought I'd come in early in case you needed help getting ready for the meeting. Where's Debbie?" she asked.

"She was mugged last night. She's home and all right now, but she's going to take a day or two off to rest," Andrew said.

"Oh, that's awful! Well I'm happy to help you with the quarterly meeting. I'm sure I can jump into Debbie's shoes with no problem," Theresa said confidently.

She completely ignored the fact that Patty stood by Andrew's side and he found himself mildly annoyed at how oblivious she could be.

He knew he shouldn't be. She was new to the team and trying to prove herself and she was only trying to help. But he was on edge after what had happened to Debbie.

"Oh, thank you, but that's not necessary. We have shadow assistants in place for all the corporate officers. Patty always knows everything Debbie is doing and is prepped and ready to jump into Debbie's role if needed. It won't be an issue."

He turned to Patty. "Can you unlock the conference room and double check that everything was set out last night? The continental breakfast should be set up by eight o'clock."

"I assume Jim's Deli is delivering?" Patty asked.

"Yes. Will you keep an eye out for them? I didn't call and tell their delivery guy to ask for you instead of Debbie," Andrew said as he headed down the hall to his office.

"No problem," Patty said as she headed toward the conference room.

Neither Andrew nor Patty noticed that Theresa stood with her hands fisted tight, nails digging into the palms of her hands. If looks could kill, Patty would be dead in her tracks.

Theresa took a deep breath and unfurled her fists. Looking down, she saw that there were small crescents turning red with blood where her nails had cut.

She took deep breaths, just as her doctor had taught her to years before. In and out. In and out. Deep, calming breaths.

There was a time when Theresa would have really lost it in a situation like this. Back before her sessions with Dr. Baker, she would have needed to hide in a bathroom and cut herself. She would have watched as the small lines of beautiful magenta raised up on her pale skin, replacing the pain and rage she felt.

She was healthier now. She no longer needed to cut. She was able to breathe and calm herself instead.

Just another problem to be tackled.

If Theresa was good at anything, it was fixing problems. She always prided herself on finding the right solution.

I'll just address Patty next. That's all. Take things one step at a time, one problem at a time, working closer and closer to Andrew. Then he'll see. He'll see me and remember we're meant for each other. Meant to be together like no one else.

CHAPTER 24

Jill spent the morning in her darkroom. She occasionally shot with a digital camera and she used digital for her marketing photos. But for most of her artwork, she still used film. Good old-fashioned film that she developed in her darkroom.

She loved developing her shots the old-fashioned way. The smell of chemicals, the click of the reel as she loaded film for processing, the ability to play with her shots by dodging or burning areas of the picture or using different filters.

These things made Jill fall in love with the art of photography and she wouldn't give them up for the convenience of a digital camera and computer.

She came out of the darkroom she'd set up in her grandparents' basement and checked her messages. She always turned the ringer off when she was developing so she could focus on her work, getting the timing and exposures just right. Jill knew that when she lost her focus, she wasted materials and time.

There were no voicemails but there was a text from Andrew asking Jill to call him. She almost laughed at the small thrill she got from seeing his text. She dialed his number as she walked up the stairs and went to the back door to let Rev out for a potty break.

"Hey, gorgeous!" came Andrew's voice over the line. She felt a shiver of excitement rip through her, as if his hands tripped over her body, setting off all of her erogenous zones.

"Hey, yourself, sexy."

"Oh, I could get used to being called sexy," came his deep reply. "You're good for my ego." Jill could hear Andrew's smile through the phone.

"Ha! As if you need any help with that ego, mister. Now, why are you chatting me up during the day instead of working?"

"What are your plans this weekend? Thursday night through Sunday afternoon," he clarified.

"What are you up to?" she asked, suspicion lacing her tone.

She wasn't at all sure she wanted to be making weekend plans with Andrew. She could already feel the pull of a 'real' relationship with him, but wasn't sure she wanted to let this go past the no-strings sex stage.

Hell, who was she kidding? It was already past that stage, but she still felt the need to dig in her heels and fight it if she could. Andrew had told her he didn't do strings. If she couldn't keep this relationship casual, she knew she'd end up hurt.

"Would you be okay with letting Kelly and Jack keep Rev for you for the weekend?" He still wasn't giving Jill a clue about what he was getting at.

"Maybe... What are you planning, Andrew?" She tried to put censure in her tone but it was hard to be tough with Andrew. He was too damn cute, and he knew it.

"I have to go to Austin, Texas for a meeting Friday but I'll finish early in the afternoon. I thought if you came with me, we could head out to Big Bend National Park afterward. It's a long drive but if we fly out of Midland-Odessa instead of driving back to Austin, we should be able to spend Saturday and some of

Sunday morning hiking. You'll get some great pictures and there's a resort and spa we can stay at nearby."

She could hear the excitement in his voice as he detailed their plans. That and the fact that he would go out of his way to bring her somewhere for her photography, rather than just viewing her photography as an afterthought, melted her resolve in an instant. Not to mention her heart.

She was surprised she wasn't a puddle on the floor after hearing the way he had planned this side trip for her.

"I'll tell Rev to pack his bags," she said. She didn't try to hide the excitement in her voice. "Did you already call Kelly or should I call her?"

"I talked to her earlier so I'll just tell Jack to let her know. Kelly was excited to have built in entertainment for the puppy all weekend. Your dog has his work cut out for him."

"Oh, Rev will love it. As long as Kelly pays Rev in treats, he'll be happy."

"I'll make the reservations. See you tonight? I can bring take out," he said.

It really wasn't necessary for him to ask at this point. It had become a given that they would have dinner and spend the evenings together. The only real question each night was whether they would go out or stay in. Apparently tonight, Andrew wanted to stay in and that suited Jill just fine.

"See you then," she said with a smile that she couldn't fight off if she tried.

As she pocketed her phone, she heard it ring again.

"What'd you forget?" Jill asked. Figuring it was Andrew, she hadn't bothered to look at the screen. There was a heavy pause before she heard a voice she hadn't expected and wasn't happy to hear.

"Jill? It's Jake. Who were you expecting?"

She swallowed a sigh. "What can I do for you, Jake?"

"No need to sound so formal. I just wanted to see how you are."

"Jake, I've asked you to leave me alone. I mean it. I don't want to talk to you, don't want to hear from you and don't want to tell you how I am. I asked for a clean break. You need to respect that," she said. She gave up trying and let the exasperation boil over and pour through the phone.

"I don't understand why you're so upset with me for checking up on you. I still care about how you're doing. I want to know that you're okay," he said.

He really sounds like he believes his own crap.

"Jake, you're the last person who has the right to ask how I'm doing. You gave up that right when you left our bed for another woman's. You don't get to care about how I am. You don't get to call. You don't get to check up on me. You get nothing, period."

She pressed the 'end' button and turned off her phone. So much for the smile Andrew had put on her face. Jill was just about to stomp back to the darkroom when it dawned on her.

She wasn't hurt and sad and angry. She wasn't filled with heartache and loss like she had been every time she spoke to Jake in the past.

This time, she was ticked off and frustrated. She was agitated and annoyed.

But that was it. No more heartbreak. Jill's smile returned as she slid the door to her darkroom open and went back to her chemicals.

CHAPTER 25

Andrew finished his Friday meeting just after lunch and picked Jill up at the hotel. He insisted on first class tickets for the flight and had set up appointments for Jill at the spa to keep her entertained Friday morning.

After the spa, she spent the rest of the time during Andrew's meetings walking the trail at Lady Bird Lake in Austin enjoying the sixty-degree weather that was such a change from the New England cold.

The trail was just off the hotel grounds and she caught several shots of eight or more turtles at a time bathing in the sun on logs out on the water. The turtles were the size of basketballs, layered one over the other in a long row as they sunbathed.

With the sun sparkling on the water behind them and the exposed roots of the trees on the edge of the water, they created beautiful pictures. Jill was glad she'd grabbed her telephoto lenses when she decided to head out for her walk. She thought she'd only need the lenses for catching shots of larger animals at Big Bend, but the turtles would be great for her notecard line.

Andrew collected Jill in the rental car in the afternoon and they headed out across Texas to Big Bend National Park. During the drive he filled the time with stories of Jack's and his escapades during school.

He also gave her a more detailed version of Jack and Kelly's story and told her about Kelly's kidnapping, a story Jill had only heard an overview of before.

Several hours into the drive, she gasped at the vision of the sun beating down on a landscape of red rocks with blue sky behind and cacti in the foreground. Without even asking if Jill wanted him to, Andrew pulled the car over so that she could get out and take pictures.

He waited patiently while she changed lenses, checked lighting and switched apertures to achieve different effects she could play with in the darkroom later.

When she was finished, she turned back around to find Andrew leaning on the hood of the car. His long legs were out in front of him, ankles crossed, eyes on her as she walked toward him.

Jill leaned in and kissed Andrew, feeling the sparks start to fly as she pressed the full length of her body to his. He brought his arms slowly up her back, pulling her even closer until she was anchored between his legs. She was pressed as close as Andrew could manage and she loved it.

"What was that for?" he asked when they broke the heated kiss.

"For being patient," she said, but she knew in her heart it was for so much more.

"I like watching you work," he said. "It's sexy." His grin was devilish.

They climbed back into the car and Jill's heart did a little flip when Andrew used the word 'work' to describe her photography.

"You're so intense and focused and you bite your bottom lip when you find something you really want to capture. Makes me want to bite your bottom lip...and other parts of you." He threw a grin her way that had her blushing.

She studied him as he pulled the car back out onto the road and continued toward their destination.

"What?" he asked in response to Jill's scrutiny.

"I'm just not used to it, that's all."

"To someone caring about you and your work? Respecting what you do?" he asked, as if he knew the answer.

She nodded and Andrew bit out his usually refrain about her ex.

"Jackass."

Jill laughed. For the first time, she felt glad Jake had left her. She might not have a future with Andrew, but she was content.

And even though Andrew had helped bring her to that new state of happiness, she didn't feel like she relied on him for the peace she was feeling. She was beginning to feel more comfortable with herself. She was confident and satisfied with life lately. That made enjoying her time with Andrew that much easier to do.

She settled back for the rest of the trip, leaning back in her seat and watching the road in front of them. They drove in silence for a while; the kind of comfortable silence that neither felt driven to break or fill simply for the sake of it. When Andrew spoke, his tone was serious for the first time in the trip.

"Do you still want it? Family? Love? Kids?"

Jill felt a kick in her gut at the question and measured her response. "I do. The only problem is that I no longer believe that love can be lasting and I can't figure out a way around that. And, I know Jake was an ass, at best." she stopped and grinned at Andrew, acknowledging the reference to Jake's ass-ness once again.

"But..." She took a shaky breath and continued. "When we got married, we were in love. It just died somewhere along the way. I honestly don't know how I would trust in love again or trust that my husband wouldn't leave again. I think I'd walk around waiting for the other shoe to drop all the time."

Jill was quiet for a minute before she continued. "With Jake, I was so sure, so confident of our love and our marriage until the day I was completely blindsided. I don't want to be blindsided like that again. I don't think I could handle that."

"Why didn't you guys have kids?" Andrew asked.

"We almost did. We waited a few years before trying so we could just enjoy being married to one another for a while. Three years in, I got pregnant but I lost the baby in my tenth week."

Her voice broke slightly as she said the words. She hadn't spoken of her baby in a long time. Hadn't told very many people about it.

"I'm sorry, honey." Andrew reached over and threaded her fingers in his and she smiled at him.

"It was hard at the time, but I guess I just think it must have been meant to be. Now that things worked out the way they did with Jake, it's a relief not to have kids involved. It would be horrible for them to be caught between us."

"Did you guys try again after that?" Andrew asked. He kept his eyes on the road even though there wasn't much to keep an eye out for in the wide-open space.

"No. Jake said he couldn't watch me go through that again. Looking back, I think that was an excuse. I don't think Jake wanted kids." Jill saw everything about her marriage through a new lens now that she was on the outside.

"Can you...I mean?" Andrew started but didn't seem to know how to ask what he wanted to know.

She filled in for him. "Have kids? Yes, I think so. The doctor said he saw no reason for me to miscarry again. Some women just lose a baby for no identifiable reason but then go on to have several children without any issues. Of course, that would mean either doing it on my own or trusting someone else again."

"Do you think you would ever have a child on your own?" he asked.

"I don't know. I haven't given it much thought." She frowned. "I wanted that baby so much at the time."

She didn't say anymore and Andrew stopped questioning, letting them slip comfortably back into the silence.

At sunset, they stopped again so she could capture the sun setting over the horizon. They pulled off the highway for dinner at a restaurant before checking in at the resort and spa for the night. The conversation had returned to light-hearted banter and easier topics than the heaviness of marriage and the shared anguish of lost children.

CHAPTER 26

When it hit Andrew it hit him hard. So hard, he was sure he might have been knocked off balance if not for the large boulder he leaned on as he watched Jill photograph the stunning canvas of Big Bend National Park.

He loved Jill. He almost laughed at the realization of that. Laughed at the fact he hadn't seen it until that moment. How could he have missed it?

In such a short time, Jill had crept into his heart and laid claim to it and he had been powerless to defend himself against her. The funniest part of it was that he didn't mind at all. He wasn't in a panic like he thought he would be. Andrew was completely calm while the emotion washed over him as he watched her.

Even so, he sure as hell couldn't tell Jill he loved her. That, for damned sure, wasn't gonna happen. And it surprised him to realize it wasn't his own fears that stood in the way. He wouldn't be afraid to tell Jill he loved her because of his own baggage. No. The problem was with her hearing it.

He knew Jill would run like hell if he mentioned love. She was too gun-shy after her marriage. But he did need to figure out how to convince her to spend the rest of her life with him without actually telling her the truth – any other result would leave him broken again.

He couldn't conceive of a life without her by his side. Without her smile and those smoky, smoldering eyes and the laughter he loved to hear. Without her sexy, sensual kisses that knocked him on his ass and without waking up to find her in his arms.

She turned to Andrew with a smile that pulled him out of his musing.

"You must be bored to tears," she said apologetically.

If only she knew.

"Nope. Not at all. I like the surroundings and the view is… exceptional," he said as he looked straight at her. "Besides, I like watching you work. I can tell that you'll pull images out of here that I wouldn't have spotted for all the world. It'll be incredible to see what you bring home and to know I was there and missed all the nuances you spotted. It's like you have a different set of eyes and you'll show me, let me in on all the secrets, when we get you home to your darkroom."

Jill stared at him with eyes wide and her mouth forming a small O.

"What?" he asked with a laugh.

She shook her head. "You always say things that make me feel so special. How do you do that? You know the right thing, just the right thing, to say all the time – even if I didn't know what I needed to hear until after it was out of your mouth."

He grinned and pulled her into his arms for a long kiss then rested his forehead on hers. "What can I say? You bring it out in me," he teased.

He wanted to keep things light as his mind churned up a plan to convince Jill to overlook her fear of love and stay with him forever.

With all the strength she could manage, Jill was fighting to keep from falling head over heels for Andrew. The man was not making it easy on her. He went hiking through the park with her, waited patiently for over two hours while she watched a family of black bears until they came close enough to capture photos through her telephoto lens.

Then he hiked higher into the hills with her to try to spot a mountain lion, based on reports of a sighting in that area the previous day.

And now, as she lay in his arms in bed trying to catch her breath and to steady herself, she could scarcely remember her name. He had tormented and tortured her in the most sensual, delicious ways.

He began with those hot, drug-like kisses that swept her under instantly, making her knees weak, her mind foggy. After bringing her almost to orgasm with his hands and tongue, he plunged into her, filling her for a few heady, perfect strokes and then pulled out only to begin his ministrations with hands and tongue all over again.

Andrew had played with her, repeatedly burying himself in her only long enough to have her begging for release over and over until she was coiled tight as a spring and ready to explode.

When he finally pushed her over the edge, she had tumbled into a climax that strummed and pulsed through her whole body in a way she never felt before and, was ashamed to admit, would beg for again and again.

She no longer thought about her ex-husband and how unsatisfying her sex life had been with Jake. Now that Jill had a point of reference, her only thoughts were on Andrew and the places he took her when they were in bed together.

She couldn't allow herself to fall for him emotionally, but she would permit herself to wallow in the magic of his hands, his mouth, his body, for as long as she could. That much she could give herself. And him.

CHAPTER 27

Andrew lay holding Jill in his arms, his hands idly running patterns up and down the smooth, creamy skin of her torso. He had never experienced anything like the pleasure he found in her arms.

And as he held her, it suddenly became crystal clear. He knew how to convince her to marry him. How to build a life with Jill forever.

Andrew had to be clinical about it. Logical and practical. Because if the topic of love came up, he was confident she would run.

It was staggering how perfect a fit they were for one another. Andrew, who thought he would never risk saying those words again, and Jill, who could never stand to hear them again. Taking a deep breath, he set out to fit the pieces of their perfect puzzle together, without sending her into flight.

"We should get married, Jill," he said, not stopping the strumming of his hands across her body.

She moved in a flash. She suddenly stood completely naked at the foot of the bed looking at him as if he had two heads. She was so incredibly beautiful.

So, so... Andrew couldn't think of a word to describe Jill's beauty. There just weren't words for how she looked standing there with nothing covering her except for a look of incredulity.

He chuckled and held out his hand to her, calling her back to bed. "Calm down, honey. Come listen to me. You'll see I'm right."

She gaped at him and shook her head. She didn't come back to bed.

"Really, Jillie, come here. You'll get cold standing there like that," he coaxed, with a pointed look down the length of her naked body.

She looked down as if she had forgotten her naked state and yelped before jumping back onto the bed. She wrapped herself in one of the sheets, but didn't wrap herself back in Andrew's arms.

She stayed on the other side of the bed, eyeing him suspiciously. She still hadn't said a word, so he plunged into his pitch.

"Think about it. We're perfect together. We both still want a family, a good marriage, even though we can't exactly trust in love the way most people might. But we're great friends, we more than enjoy each other's company, and we're great in bed together. Our chemistry is...well, phenomenal, to say the least," he said with a grin.

"I...I can't, Andrew. I can't go through that again," she protested.

He held up a hand, palm out to her. "Hear me out. I'll give you a guarantee. A penalty clause to keep you feeling safe. I'll have my lawyers draw up a prenup that gives you everything I have, every ounce of my money and property if I leave you at any point.

"That's millions, Jill. A *lot* of millions." He didn't tell her it was actually a little over two billion. He knew she'd freak. "I'd even lose Adelaide. The only way the marriage would end would be if you wanted it to end. Not me. You'll never have to worry about being blindsided again."

He could see the temptation pulling at her, but she remained wary. She shook her head silently for a moment.

"What about you, Andrew? What guarantees would you have?" she asked.

"I don't need guarantees from you, Jill. I've known you half my life. I know you'd never hurt me the way Blair did. I know you wouldn't, hell, couldn't even contemplate the kind of cruelty she displayed. It's just not in you to do something like that."

He took a breath and then threw in the biggest lure of all. "We can try to have kids, Jill. And if you can't, we'll adopt, but I bet we can. And, we'd be good parents together, because we have a good friendship as our foundation. We're good together, Jill. We're good *for* each other."

By now, he had coaxed her back to his side and his hands began their soothing play over her back, her arms and shoulders. The two of them lay quietly like that for a long time. Andrew barely breathing. Jill thinking so hard it was almost audible.

"Yes."

She said it so quietly, he wasn't sure she'd actually spoken. Just the quietest whisper of 'yes' and his heart kicked over in his chest.

He pulled her back and looked into her eyes. "Yes?"

She nodded. "Yes, I'll marry you."

He closed his eyes and pulled her close, reveling in the power of that one word.

It wasn't traditional or romantic or any of the things that a proposal should be – and that tore at Andrew's heart because he wanted more than anything in the world, to give Jill all of those things and more – but it was what she needed it to be.

And from that moment on, Andrew knew he would always put her needs above his own. He would forever do whatever it took to keep Jill happy.

CHAPTER 28

*A*ndrew returned to the office Monday ready to share his good news, only to face another surprising blow. Patty had been hit in a hit-and-run accident on Friday night. It happened right in the parking garage connected to the building where Sutton Capital leased its office space.

Patty was in stable condition but she suffered numerous broken bones and a concussion. She hadn't seen much. Only a dark sedan. The driver seemed to be bending over the passenger seat as if they were reaching for something. Two seconds of the driver's inattention caused such pain for Patty. Thankfully, her injuries were not life-threatening and her recovery would be complete.

The worst part of all was that the driver didn't pull over. The person left Patty there in the parking lot to be found by the security patrol. Video surveillance of the exit showed only a black sedan with the license plate missing on the front of the car and covered by mud on the back. The driver wore a hat and could not be seen clearly in the fuzzy tape.

For the second time in a week, Andrew was grim as he sent flowers to one of his staff to encourage a speedy recovery. At least Debbie was back at work and seemed to be feeling fine, if a bit stiff. It made Andrew feel marginally better to see Debbie up and around.

"Hey, guys," Andrew said as he walked into Jack's office to meet with Chad and Jack.

"Hey, how was the trip?" Jack asked.

Andrew grinned. He had planned to wait to tell them until he and Jill could tell everyone together, but what the hell? He couldn't get the smile off his face or hide his happiness, so why not tell his best friends?

"Jill and I are getting married." It felt weird to say it and by the shocked looks on his friends' faces, it sounded a little funny too.

"Holy shit! We send you off for the weekend, a confirmed bachelor, and you come back ready to tie the knot," Chad said.

Jack just grinned and shook Andrew's hand, pulling him in for a one-armed hug.

"I love her. It just hit me one day. I just can't picture life without her," Andrew said.

Jack got a funny look on his face. "Did you tell her that?" he asked.

Andrew and Jack had talked about Andrew's feelings about confessing love to someone.

"Oh, hell no. I wanted to but she'd freak if I told her that." Andrew heard groans from both of his friends but continued on. "Jill's not really in a place to hear that. She was in love with her husband and thought her husband was in love with her. After the way that ended, she says she won't put her faith in love again. She would run if I told her how I feel."

"So, how exactly did this proposal go?" Chad asked, scrubbing a hand over the back of his neck.

"It's complicated," Andrew said, fighting not to squirm under their scrutiny.

This earned him hard, level stares from both his friends.

Andrew shrugged. "Look, all you need to know is that we're

great friends, the chemistry is off the charts, and we want a life together. We *both* want a future together. That's all that matters. How I got us there isn't important."

Jack was the first to diffuse the tension. "Hey, far be it from me to judge. I paid my wife to marry me and look how happy we are. If this is what you want, I'm happy for you, man."

"Yeah, Jack's right. Congratulations, little guy." In light of his unusual height and size, Chad called Jack and Andrew 'little guy' fairly often.

The clap on the back told Andrew Chad was trying to lighten the mood.

Jack grabbed a bottle of Scotch from a drawer and poured each of them two fingers to toast Andrew's good news before they settled down to begin their morning meeting.

Just before lunchtime, Jennie was surprised to hear that all staff were being called for an impromptu employee meeting in the front lobby. This wasn't anything she'd ever seen at Sutton Capital. She tried to catch Chad to ask him what was going on, but she didn't see him anywhere.

She walked to the front lobby and took a spot at the edge of the group waiting for Jack to begin the meeting.

"I know this is a bit unusual, guys," Jack began in the informal way he often addressed the close-knit team at Sutton. "But we have a few things to celebrate today. First, I want to welcome back Debbie, who assures me she's feeling better than ever."

Amidst the clapping and good-natured welcome back messages from those around her, Jennie heard a harsh whisper next to her.

"What is *she* doing back?" Jennie turned to see Theresa's pinched face next to her.

"Um, I guess she's ready to come back?" Jennie was never at a loss for words. Except around Theresa. Something about this woman just wasn't right. Moments later, her theory was confirmed when Jennie saw Theresa's response to Jack's second announcement.

"And, congratulations are in order for Andrew as well," Jack continued when the room quieted down. "Andrew and his girlfriend, Jill, got engaged this weekend. Join me in wishing them a long and happy life together!"

This time the room exploded in talk and cheers as all of Sutton Capital lined up to celebrate with Andrew. In the middle of clapping her hands, Jennie felt Theresa's hand clench down on her arm in a crushing grip.

"I thought you said he had only been dating that woman for a short time? Why would he be marrying her?" Theresa spit her words out.

Jennie stared at the woman next to her and then wrenched her arm free. She rubbed the spot where Theresa's hand had gripped her arm, sure there would be bruises tomorrow.

Every instinct Jennie had was raised as she watched the look of rage on Theresa's face and heard a mumbled accusation of pregnancy to trap a man.

"Excuse me, I need to go to lunch," Jennie said, anxious to get away from Theresa.

"Oh, great, I'll go with you. We can talk more," Theresa said.

"No!" Jennie shot out before realizing how her response sounded. "I mean, I have a lunch meeting I have to get to."

Just then Chad walked by. Jennie hoped Chad would understand her signal when she reached out and grabbed his bicep as he walked past.

"Chad, are you ready for our lunch meeting?" she asked. She felt Chad's arm tense under her hand, but he didn't miss a beat.

"You bet. If you're ready now, that works for me," Chad said. He put a protective hand on Jennie's lower back and walked with her to the elevator.

CHAPTER 29

As soon as the elevator doors closed, Chad turned to Jennie. He rubbed his hands up and down her arms as he studied her face.

"You okay?" Chad asked softly.

Jennie nodded, unable to speak.

Any other time, his attention would have her heart speeding up. But today, nothing could puncture the unease she was feeling.

"Gonna tell me what that was about?" He raised an eyebrow and waited, his voice soft, reassuring.

"Something's wrong with that woman, Chad. She's scary. And really, really focused on Andrew."

Now Chad was all business. "What woman?"

Jennie recounted the odd way Theresa talked about Andrew. The weird questions about Jill and his engagement. The creepy feeling she got whenever she was around Theresa.

Jennie didn't mention the way Theresa had grabbed her or the fact that she suspected her arm was already bruising. She kept her sleeves down and her mouth shut.

If Chad heard that, he'd likely fire Theresa on the spot and Jennie knew firing someone had to be well documented and done carefully to avoid repercussions. Jennie didn't want her creepy feelings about Theresa to come back to haunt Sutton Capital if she said something to make Chad act too rashly.

"Are you going out on assignment this week, Jen?" Chad asked when she had finished telling him about Theresa.

"No. I'm in house for the rest of the month," she said.

"Good. Consider Theresa your assignment. When we get back, I want you to write down what just happened. See if you can get close to her. Let me know if you see or hear anything unusual. And document everything. I'll fill Jack and the head of Human Resources in on your assignment but other than the four of us, let's keep it quiet."

Jennie nodded.

"Come to me with any concern. If she has you at all worried, if you don't feel safe, you come to me. Got it?" Chad instructed.

"Got it, Boss."

"Good." Chad grinned as they stepped out into the lobby. "Now let's get that lunch."

CHAPTER 30

The next few weeks passed in a whirlwind for Jill. Andrew surprised her with a stunning ring. The thin band was inlaid with diamonds and a large round yellow diamond was set in the center and surrounded by more white diamonds. Jill didn't think she would have been able to pick a ring more suited to her sense of style if she had tried. The fact that Andrew chose something so perfect for her took her breath away.

His attorney had, in fact, written up a prenuptial agreement with the 'penalty clause' written in. It had taken quite a bit of insistence to get his lawyer not only to do it, but also make it iron-clad, but in the end Andrew had gotten what he wanted. He also asked Jill to have her lawyer look over it to be sure it was done right.

Andrew and Jill announced their engagement to friends and family. Nora wanted to host an engagement party but they convinced her they wanted the affair to be more quiet and private. For once, Nora backed down.

They set the date for spring. Since it was nearly Thanksgiving now, that gave Jill plenty of time to plan things. She wanted a small wedding, with both the ceremony and the reception at

Nora's house. Andrew still needed to sell his downtown condo and find a house they both liked, but there was time for that, too. And, with the way their tastes so often meshed, Jill had no concerns on that front – she was certain she and Andrew would find something easily.

They began to spend their weekends at the ski cabin that Andrew, Jack, Chad and some of their other friends from grad school all owned together in Vermont. The group had bought the cabin back when they were still in school.

Even though most of the group had plenty of family money and easily could have bought the cabin through their families, the friends had insisted on using their own money on it and sharing the expense.

At the time, they didn't have much money of their own, so there were a total of six of them that each owned a share.

Now that many of the owners were getting married and starting to think about children – or in the case of Jack and Kelly who had just announced they already had children on the way – they had plans for each of the owners to build their own ski cabin on the property in the next few years. They'd leave the original cabin as a place for guests to stay. To that end, they had bought up additional property on the mountain and now owned the upper two thirds.

One of the group, an architect, had begun to work on plans for the new cabins.

Most weekends in the winter months, all or some of the six and their significant others could be found there. Jill loved the weekends at the cabin. She trekked through the woods on snowshoes with her cameras while Andrew skied.

They spent the evenings surrounded by good friends and laughter. She felt wonderful enveloped by so much love and couldn't believe the way Andrew's friends all opened up to her instantly. She felt content and happy there.

In fact, Jill felt content and happy all the time now. When she was with Andrew, things just felt right. She felt cherished and appreciated and valued in a way she hadn't in her marriage.

She also felt good because he seemed happy and content too – and how he felt mattered to her. She felt as though she and Andrew were more in sync with their goals and what they wanted from each other, what they wanted in life than she and Jake had ever been. There was a unique synchronicity to the life they were building together.

During her marriage, Jill had told herself it was okay when her husband didn't want to try to have another baby. Now she realized it wasn't okay with *her*. She'd been fooling herself to try to make their marriage work.

Now she could admit, she wanted to have a baby. More than one, in fact, and Andrew wanted that too. She wanted to be able to give that to him, to share that together.

Today, Jill and Kelly planned to spend the day shopping for wedding dresses before she met up with Andrew to make the drive to the ski cabin after work.

She heard Kelly honk her horn outside and grabbed her purse and her bag for the weekend before heading out the front door and climbing into her friend's car.

Since Jill and Andrew were leaving right from the appointment at the dress boutique, Kelly and Jack were going to grab Rev later. They would keep Rev overnight then bring him up when they came to the cabin tomorrow.

"Hi, Kels," Jill said as she climbed into the passenger seat of Kelly's little red BMW.

"Hi! I can't wait to get to the store. It's so exciting to be looking for a wedding dress," Kelly gushed as she pulled out of the drive.

"I know. I'm more excited than I thought I'd be. I kind of thought it wouldn't be a big deal since it's my second time around. Jake and I did the whole giant wedding thing the first time, so I don't want anything big this time, but I really can't wait to find the perfect dress."

Jill and Kelly would need to look for bridesmaids' dresses as well. Jill's best friend from college, Amy, would be her maid of honor and Kelly would be her bridesmaid. She and Andrew had decided to keep the number of attendants small, with Jack and Chad standing with Andrew.

Kelly pulled into the parking lot of the small bridal boutique where she had found her dress and she and Jill went inside. Kelly spent a few minutes catching up with Bria, the owner of the shop, before they got down to business.

"I have a bit of a different process than most bridal boutiques. I like to get to know a bit about you and the groom so I can help steer you toward the right dress for your connection. Most people think the wedding gown should only be about what the bride likes, what looks good on her, what will fit well. I promise I'll take all of that into consideration, but it should be so much more than that, don't you think?" Bria asked, expecting Jill to agree with her.

"Uh, I..." started Jill, but Bria just continued on and Kelly sat nodding encouragement.

"So, tell me about Andrew. Tell me why you love him," Bria ordered.

Jill swallowed. How could she tell them that this marriage wasn't about love? It was about safety, security, and never having to wonder if one day love would fade or passion would fizzle.

Jill couldn't tell them that. She would be mortified. She would just tell them the things *about* Andrew she loved. There were many of those, even though she couldn't ever let herself fall in love with the whole.

"Um, I love the way he thinks of my needs first, I guess?" she started, a little weakly.

Kelly and Bria both nodded and looked as though they were waiting for more.

"Um, I uh, I love the way he cares about my opinions and feelings." It was getting easier now. She was on a roll. "I love the way he calls or texts me throughout the day to see how I am. And, I love the way he sometimes just knows when I'm in a bad mood and then knows how to get me out of it before I even realize what he's doing. I love his kisses and the way it feels when he holds me."

Jill was blushing now so she stopped and stared at Bria, hoping that would be enough. Bria smiled and jumped to her feet. "Strong and steady. I know the perfect dress for such strong, steady love!" she said.

Bria ran to the back of the room, leaving Jill with only one thought. *Yes, strong and steady, that's what Andrew is.*

Jill had never seen such a crazy method for choosing a wedding dress, but the dress was perfect. A floor-length, simple sheath with tiny pearls sewn around the bodice. It was classic, abiding and endless, in a style that would never fade. It draped beautifully on Jill, accentuating her tall, slim build but still showing the curve of her hips and breasts. It was simple enough to be just right for a second marriage, but it was elegant with enough flair to make Jill feel beautiful and desirable.

As Jill and Kelly left the bridal shop, Jill continued to fight the nagging feeling that she was falling much further than she should allow herself to fall for Andrew. In fact, fighting that feeling was becoming an exhausting and hopeless endeavor.

The weekend at the cabin was a particularly fun one because all the owners were up at the same time. In addition to Chad, Jack, Kelly, Andrew, and Jill, the three other men who co-owned the cabin arrived over the course of Friday evening and Saturday morning. Cade Jeffers arrived with his girlfriend, Sylvia. Those two had arrived first and got the heat turned up and a fire burning. Cade was an architect in New York City and Sylvia was an interior designer.

Greg Burton and his wife Liz came up from Hamden. Greg

owned a consulting firm in New Haven and Liz owned a catering business. Since Liz couldn't help but cook when she was with a big crowd, she had soup simmering and dough rising for loaves of homemade bread within an hour of her arrival.

The last of the group was Trent Lang and his fiancée Deidre. They had recently relocated to Boston, where they both worked in finance.

Jill had become friends with the group in the short time she'd known them. Even though she was a bit of an outsider since they'd all known each other for so much longer, they were all warm and welcoming people and she felt relaxed with them.

Jack and Kelly brought Rev up when they arrived Saturday. Jill loved to see how happy Rev was wrestling with Zoe, running in the snow, and letting everyone spoil him with tummy rubs and ear scratches. He got a few too many table scraps and treats over the weekend but it made her happy to see him so content.

It also tugged at her heart to see how happy Rev and Andrew were to see one another. Andrew seemed to have adopted Rev in his heart and the dog didn't object to that at all.

The only niggling seeds of doubt came at the end of the weekend when Cade pulled out the plans he was working on to build each of the partners their own cabins. As Jill listened to him outline the plan for the property, she began to feel uncomfortable with the idea that this special place of Andrew's – a place he shared with such close friends – would now be tied up in their penalty clause. She didn't think she could stomach the idea of taking anything so close to his heart and using it to tie him to her forever.

Andrew met Jill's eyes across the room and, as always, seemed to read her mind. Crossing the room, he wrapped his arms around her and looked into her eyes.

"What's wrong, sweetheart?" he whispered softly.

She frowned as she tried to find words to explain. "It just

seems wrong. I can't take this from you. We can't put this in the penalty clause."

Andrew looked over his shoulder at the others in the room and then pulled Jill down the hall and into their bedroom and shut the door.

∽

Andrew looked at Jill and tried to read the emotions on her face. She looked agitated. Sad. Guilty. There were too many emotions playing over her beautiful features.

"What do you mean? Everything goes in the clause." He stood in front of Jill with his arms crossed as if immovable.

She shook her head. "No, Andrew. This place is too special to you. It's for you and your friends. I don't want it in the clause."

She looked like she was close to tears and he struggled to reassure her. He knew the truth. He knew that he loved her. That his love was the reason he would never leave, not some clause in a contract, not the material things he had picked up along the way in life. The material things meant nothing next to her.

But he couldn't risk losing Jill by telling her how he felt. If he said the words and she got spooked and ran, he might not get her back.

With his hands on her upper arms, he gave a firm squeeze. "No, Jill. It's all or nothing. Everything goes in the clause. I'm not worried about losing it. Don't you see? I'm never leaving. I'll never walk away. That's the point. You can believe in that with all your heart."

"But––" she began.

"No. No buts, Jill. That clause will never come into play. I'm here forever."

She nodded and let him kiss her, wrap her in his arms. But Andrew wasn't sure she truly believed him. If he could ensure that everything went into the clause, maybe she would begin to believe. Maybe someday she would relax again.

He even, stupidly, let himself hope that maybe she could begin to fall in love with him someday. That someday she might feel the way he did and not run from that emotion. Not leave him the minute she realized the depths of her feelings.

CHAPTER 31

*J*ill kept an eye on Rev as she refilled the bird feeders in her front yard. As usual, the dog was racing around the yard without a care in the world. If she hoped to spot any birds later today, she'd need to keep him in the house long enough for the birds to come out of hiding.

She almost dropped the bag of birdseed a minute later when she heard Rev's deep barking. His happy barks were higher pitched, but once in a blue moon, Rev found something that needed to be warned off and then his deep, growling bark came out with threatening force. Like now.

Jill looked up at the unusual sight of Rev standing at the front of the yard. His whole body was launched, hackles up, teeth bared as he barked at someone in a car.

"Rev, come!" Jill called out as she started jogging toward him. The yard was deep, the house set back from the road, and that made it hard for her to make out the person in the car. *A woman?* The car started and drove off, leaving the dog barking behind it.

As the car pulled away, Rev circled back to Jill, but he didn't calm down. He stood with one back foot on her foot like he could protect her by pinning her in place, body still coiled and ready as he watched the spot where the car had been.

"What was that all about, big guy?" Jill crouched and stroked his chest. His whole body was still tense.

Andrew came up behind her.

"What was that about? I heard him from up in the bedroom." He'd been sleeping in while Jill and Rev filled the bird feeders.

"I don't know. He gets protective on very rare occasions but never anything like that. He's a Labradoodle, for heaven's sake, not a guard dog. I don't know what brought that on." She gazed up at Andrew, confused.

"Did you see who it was?" Andrew asked.

"A woman? Maybe? I couldn't see much. I didn't notice the car at all until Rev started barking. Probably nothing. Someone visiting a neighbor or something."

Andrew drew Jill into his arms, sending tingles of anticipation through her body and quickly erasing thoughts of the strange car and driver from her mind.

"Let's go back to bed," he whispered in her ear as he nuzzled her neck.

He took her hands and tugged her back toward the house.

"Come on Revil, Devil, Demon Child. Let's go!" Andrew called out and the dog dropped into place beside them, following them back into the house like any of those words were actually his name.

Fucking dog. Great, now I need to research sedatives for dogs. Or maybe, just kill the damn thing. Rat poison? I wonder how much rat poison I'd have to hide in a steak to kill a dog that size.

Theresa drove away from the barking dog and pulled down the street. No wonder that whore had her claws in Andrew. They lived next door to each other and, from what Theresa had been able to find out, their families had been close for a long time.

Hell, Andrew was probably expected to marry her like in some archaic arranged marriage. He didn't have a choice.

Theresa sighed. Sometimes it really sucked to be in love with a man from old money. They had weird customs and expectations. This might make it harder to wrestle Andrew out of the whore's clutches but Theresa could be patient. She'd come up with a plan. Until the right time, she'd wait and gather information.

Theresa drove home and went back to work on her computer, sorting through newspaper stories for information on Andrew and Jill, looking up property records and trying to uncover more of Andrew's holdings and accounts. The more information she collected, the better prepared she'd be when Andrew needed her.

I'm working on it, my beautiful Andrew. Just be patient and I'll have us together soon.

CHAPTER 32

*A*s time passed, Jill realized that Andrew had not only helped her regain her confidence, he'd brought it to new heights. Just before the holidays, the entire Sutton Capital team spent the night in New York City at a fundraising event. The event raised money for a charity sponsored by one of the companies Sutton Capital had a big hand in starting. Jill put her newfound confidence to work to turn the tables on Andrew.

She excused herself from the large round table in one of the Ritz-Carlton Hotel ballrooms where a group of them were eating, and headed to the ladies' room. Moments later, she walked back across the ballroom, with the small red thong panties she had been wearing under her silk gown balled up in her fist.

As Jill found her seat again, she brushed a kiss across Andrew's cheek and pressed the scrap of lace and silk into his hand under the table. He shot her a puzzled look and then looked down and opened his hand.

Jill kept a small, polite smile on her face as she talked with Kelly and Jennie, but she saw the look on Andrew's face when he processed what she had handed him.

As their entrees were served, she slipped her hand under the table and let her fingers trail up his leg. She paused on his thigh, letting her fingers trace back and forth. Then they strayed upward...and found Andrew hard and ready for her under the table.

He leaned close, his lips brushing Jill's neck as he whispered in her ear. "You'll pay for this, sweetheart."

She tilted her head and turned an innocent smile to him before returning to the conversations around the table. She never would have tried anything like this when she was with Jake.

Heaven knows, Jake wouldn't have been able to come up with a response that sent shivers of anticipation up her spine the way Andrew's words had.

If anyone noticed that Andrew was a little distracted during dinner, they didn't say anything. She had a feeling their friends knew what was happening when Andrew took her wrap from the back of her chair just after dessert was served. He stood and took hold of her arm, her wrap strategically draped over his other arm to cover the results of Jill's dinnertime torment.

She laughed when he didn't even try to come up with an excuse for the group. "Goodnight, everyone," he said as he pulled her from the room and steered her toward the elevators in the hall.

Chad laughed as he watched Andrew lead Jill from the room, clearly intent on hauling her upstairs for a more private party of their own.

His laughter was interrupted when he felt Jennie's hand on his arm. Chad followed Jennie's gaze and cursed under his breath when he saw what Jennie spotted. Theresa stood stock still across the room watching Jill and Andrew exit the ballroom. The look on her face was pure rage. Seething, undisguised and unrepentant rage.

Chad needed to speed this up and get her out of the company and away from his friend. Fast.

CHAPTER 33

Andrew jabbed the button to call the elevator and scowled at Jill when she laughed at this predicament.

He bent to her ear and whispered, sending shivers through her body. "Laugh, sweetheart. Laugh all you want. But I'm going to love making you pay for this. And I'll take my time, baby."

When the elevator doors opened, he pulled her inside. He pushed the button for their floor, and pressed her against the wall of the elevator, crushing her lips with a kiss.

"Not nice, Jill," he said as he broke the kiss. "You've just earned yourself hours of torture and torment." Jill's dress slit up to her thigh, allowing him access. He growled when he found Jill wet and ready for him. Teasing Andrew at the table had turned into as much suffering for her as it was for him.

As he stroked her , using his body to cover what he was doing between them from cameras, he nipped at her neck and continued to whisper in her ear. "By the time I'm finished with you, sweet Jill, you'll never misbehave again. You'll be begging me to let you come and promising to be on your best behavior if I'll just give you that sweet relief you need."

Jill groaned, knowing Andrew could make good on that threat. When they got to their room, he did just that. Somehow, he managed to call on a level of patience and control like Jill had never seen. He used his hands, his mouth, his teeth, to drive her close to the edge, but always pulled back just before she toppled over to the release she needed.

"Please, Andrew, please," she cried as he pulled back yet again.

He laughed, low and sexy deep in his throat. "I told you I'd make you pay."

"I need you inside me, Andrew. Please, I need you now." She raised her hips, trying to rock against him, to urge him to fill her, but he pulled back, having none of it.

"Promise to be a good girl?"

"No." She writhed under him.

"I'm sorry, sweetheart. You have to be taught a lesson."

Desperate, she pulled out the one card she held. "Andrew, I started taking the pill two weeks ago."

He stilled, his lips still touching her inner thigh where she'd interrupted his ministrations.

She knew she had his attention.

"It takes two weeks for the pill to be effective, Andrew. Do you know what that means?"

He crawled up her body, his forearms framing her face, meeting her gaze. All the laughter was gone from his eyes. It was replaced by a look of sheer wonder that made Jill's breath catch in her throat.

"Please tell me that means what I think it means, Jill," he said.

Jill smiled and nodded. "No condom."

His groan was low in his throat as he leaned in to kiss her gently, passionately, no longer toying with her. He kept his eyes on hers, deepening his kiss.

Then slowly, tenderly, he entered her, bringing a gasp to her lips. She pressed her lips to his shoulder and bit down as he thrust into her slowly again and again, causing the sweet pressure of orgasm to build.

"Oh, Jill," he groaned. His voice seemed to fade away as if he couldn't find words.

She knew just how he felt. The feeling of being with Andrew with nothing separating them was so intimate. At that moment, she felt closer to Andrew than she'd ever felt to anyone. There were no words to describe what she was feeling physically or emotionally as they climaxed together moments later.

CHAPTER 34

The end of November came and Jill and Andrew joined family and friends for Thanksgiving at Jack and Kelly's house. They picked up Nora and Lydia and brought them along.

Chad and Chad's mother, Mabry, were already gathered and Jill was introduced to them, along with the rest of the gathered crowd. She tried to memorize faces and names. Chad was Jack's cousin and also one of Andrew's best friends.

Jennie, who also worked at Sutton, planned to stop by for dessert later in the evening. Once again, Jill found herself surrounded by love and comfort and she absorbed as much of that as she could. It felt really good to be around so much love.

Kelly's family was wonderful. Her mother and sister, Jesse, wanted to hear all about the plans for the wedding. They had some great ideas since they had just been through the wedding planning process with Jack and Kelly.

Nora and Lydia jumped into the wedding daydreams as well and Jill had to remind everyone that they wanted something small and understated. If she wasn't careful, she would end up renting out the Waldorf-Astoria in New York with five hundred of their closest friends.

In traditional Thanksgiving manner, the men gathered in the

living room to watch football. The women gravitated to the kitchen and pitched in to help Mrs. Poole, Jack and Kelly's housekeeper, finish up the Thanksgiving dinner with occasional visits from a man Jill was introduced to as Roark.

He came into the kitchen periodically asking if Mrs. Poole needed help. She'd shoo him out and return to her work, but twice Jill thought she saw the woman blush when he'd left the room.

"These pies look incredible," Jill said as she mashed potatoes. There were three pies set out on the counter. One was pumpkin, one apple, and the other pecan. She practically drooled as she tried to decide which one she wanted after the meal.

If she even had any room. There was so much food. There was not only a turkey, but also glazed ham, sweet potatoes and the mashed potatoes she was making. Green bean casserole, stuffing, gravy, homemade rolls that looked like they would melt in your mouth, and cranberries. She could feel the food coma coming on and she hadn't done more than snack on baked brie and veggies and dip so far.

"My sister made those," Kelly said and Jesse smiled at her sister.

Jill was impressed. "You like to bake?" she asked Jesse.

Jesse nodded but Kelly nudged her.

"She's being modest. She's going to be a famous pastry chef one day."

Jesse mumbled a response, but Roark came in at that moment, rubbing his stomach and saying he couldn't stand the smells coming out of the kitchen anymore.

"I need food, woman," he said as Mrs. Poole tried to push him away from the stove.

When it was time to sit down to eat, Jack asked Kelly's dad to carve the turkey and then heavily laden platters of food were passed around. Wine glasses were filled and finally grace was said before everyone began to eat.

Jill had been a bit sad she wouldn't be with her own family this Thanksgiving – she and Andrew planned to go see her parents at Christmas this year – but the minute she tasted Mrs. Poole's cornbread stuffing and turkey, more tender than even her own mother's, she forgot most of the sting of being away from home. The woman could cook.

Toward the end of the meal, Jack rose and cleared his throat to get everyone's attention. When a hush fell on the group, he began to speak.

"As all of you know, I have a lot to be thankful for this year. I found my beautiful, incredible, sexy wife and somehow convinced her to spend the rest of her life with me."

The love Jack held in his heart for Kelly shone in his eyes as he looked at her and Jill saw Kelly tear up at his words. They also raised a slight blush on Kelly's cheeks when Jack hit the word 'sexy.'

"We were blessed to get Kelly back safe when she was kidnapped. Instead of losing her and any possibility at happiness along with her, I was given a second chance – thanks to her quick thinking, Jesse's brains, Andrew, Chad and Samantha. I owe you guys everything," Jack said as he looked at them. Jack's voice was thick with emotion and Jill found herself tearing up as well.

She hadn't met Samantha yet and the woman wasn't at the Thanksgiving gathering, but Andrew had told Jill about her. She sounded like an amazing woman.

"I also have a second chance at a relationship with my Aunt Mabry, who I have missed more than I realized over the years." Jack squeezed his aunt's hand while she beamed back at him.

"And I am very happy to tell you all that Kelly and I are now expecting our first baby." The table exploded with congratulations and cheers from everyone. But Jill's heart felt a small pang and as she raised her eyes to Andrew's she saw his were locked on her as well. She knew they were both thinking about the children they lost and perhaps thinking about the children they might have in the future.

It was in that moment that Jill could no longer deny what she had been trying so desperately to push aside: she loved Andrew. With all her heart and all she was, she loved him.

As she sat, a new realization swept over her – all while she tried to keep up appearances, congratulating Kelly and Jack and nodding in agreement when Kelly's mom said how wonderful the couple's baby news was... Jill realized she couldn't marry Andrew.

She looked down at the tablecloth and blinked furiously, pushing back the tears burning in her eyes. She couldn't be in a marriage like she'd been in before. A one-sided marriage where Jill was in love but her husband was not. He'd told her their marriage wouldn't be based on love.

But it would be for her. And she'd be right back where she'd been with Jake.

The thought made her heart cleave clean in two.

It didn't matter that she believed Andrew would never leave her. What mattered was that she would always know why he stayed.

If she married Andrew, she would know he stayed true to her because of the penalty clause, the money. Not because of love. And, that, she realized was something she couldn't bear to live with.

Andrew watched Jill across the table. He knew she must feel a flash of pain at the news of Jack and Kelly's baby, but as he watched her, he knew something more was going on. He and Jill went from sharing a small, unspoken moment about their lost children, to something different.

She wouldn't meet his eye and she was quiet through the rest of the meal, as if she'd withdrawn into herself.

In between dessert and dinner, he found a moment alone with her and pulled her into his arms.

"Are you okay, sweetheart?" he whispered into her ear. He tried to let her feel how much he loved her, how much she meant to him through his embrace.

"Mmm hmm. I'm okay. Just tired." She pressed her head into his chest, laying her cheek on him.

He wanted to believe her but something felt off and he couldn't shake the feeling the rest of the evening.

They got through dessert, helped with cleanup, visited a bit more with everyone, but Andrew wanted to get Jill home. Get her back to where it was just the two of them in their own little world, a safe cocoon so he could find out what was bothering her.

They drove home with Lydia and Nora maintaining most of the conversation. Andrew dropped the two older women at Nora's and walked them up to the door, being careful with Nora since her hip had only recently been declared 'healed.'

Then he drove Jill and himself next door to her grandmother's house.

He was quiet in the car, preferring to wait until they got inside to press her for answers. Jill was sad. And he wasn't convinced it was only because she had been reminded of the baby she'd lost.

The minute he closed the front door, he opened his mouth to talk to her but she wrapped her arms around him and pressed her lips to his in a kiss of such deep longing, such sweet perfection, it almost knocked him to his knees.

"Make love to me, Andrew," she whispered against his lips, before taking his hand in hers and pulling him toward the bedroom.

Their lovemaking was sultry and sweet and seemed endless to him. But there was an emotion playing just underneath the surface that he didn't like. There was a sadness to it and as he lay in the aftermath with Jill in his arms, he suddenly knew.

She was leaving him.

"Why did that feel like goodbye, Jill?"

He felt her tears on his chest and he lifted her chin so he could see her eyes.

He knew he was right. The pain that gutted his chest and made him feel empty and broken told him he was right.

"Tell me what's going on. Tell me why you're leaving me," Andrew whispered. He was surprised how calm he sounded, when inside, he felt anything but.

He ached for Jill, ached to absorb her pain and her fear – to find a way to soothe her. But when she spoke and confirmed his fears he was desperate to make her stay.

"I can't, Andrew. I thought I could but I just can't," Jill began.

He felt so many emotions when his worst fear was confirmed. Anguish, sorrow, anger. He was ashamed to say, there was a lot of anger.

She slipped from the bed and pulled her robe on but he stayed where he was, trying to take measured breaths, to will away the urge to lash out at her for causing him this pain.

"Why, Jill? Why can't you?" His voice sounded so calm, but on the inside he was anything but.

Suddenly, despite the fact that he'd never thought of Jill as being like Blair, that was all he could think. She was leaving him just like Blair had.

He tried to remember that Jill was hurting and sad and he wanted to reach out and comfort her. But she was also the one causing him so much pain, tearing his future apart the same way Blair had. Taking away the happiness that had been in his grasp only hours before.

She shook her head as tears began to flow and she pressed her hand over her mouth. "I just can't go through that again," she said, her voice small and quiet.

His anger flared. He rose from the bed. "How could you think I would be anything like him? That I would leave you? I've done everything, *everything*, Jill, to show you I won't leave. What more can I do?"

He was yelling at her now as he pulled on his clothes in jerky, quick motions.

Fuck! How had this happened?

"I'm sorry, Andrew. There isn't anything you can do. It isn't you. I just can't do this."

He needed to get away from her before he lashed out and said something he couldn't take back. As he turned to leave, she called out his name and he turned to see her holding his ring out to him.

In a moment that would bring him unending shame later, he growled at Jill and swatted her hand away, sending the ring flying across the room. He stalked out of her house and away from the second woman to take his love and shred his heart with it.

Jill managed to hold herself up until she heard the door slam and Andrew's car pull down the driveway. Then she let the flood of tears, anguish and heartache come as she sank to the floor.

The pain she felt was so much greater than the pain she'd felt when Jake left her. How was that possible?

Rev came and crawled into her lap – all eighty pounds of him – and she fisted her hands into his soft curls, buried her face in his neck and cried.

CHAPTER 35

By the following week, Jill was fully wallowing in her misery. She'd been in the same sweats and t-shirt for days, not something she usually did.

When the doorbell rang, she glanced down at her sloppy clothes and her unshowered state but answered the door anyway.

Kelly didn't wait for an invitation. She walked inside, said 'hi' to Rev and then turned to look Jill up and down. "You're a mess, honey. A hot mess."

"I know." Jill couldn't really deny that. "I just love Andrew so much, it hurts to breathe without him."

Kelly shook her head and then looked at the ceiling in frustration. "Okay, you need to start from the beginning. Why did you end things if you love him? You guys were getting married, so in theory – in the absence of some scheme to get around a clause in a will like Jack and I when we were married – it's a good thing to be in love with the man you plan to spend the rest of your life with."

Jill sank down onto the couch and curled her feet under her. When Rev lay down on the floor near Jill, Kelly took her place at the other end of the couch and Jill launched into the whole story.

"So," she concluded, "when I finally realized I'd fallen in love with him, I just couldn't go through with the marriage. He's always shown he cared about me. I know Andrew cares a hell of a lot more than Jake did, but that's just not enough. I can't go into a marriage that's going to be so one-sided again."

Kelly reached over and squeezed her friend's hand. "You know what I think? I have a feeling with Jake, you found a man who was perfectly willing to tell you he loved you, even though he didn't. And I think with Andrew, you found a man who can love you but can't tell you. I've seen the way he looks at you. I see love when you guys are together, but from what Jack tells me, Blair really did a number on him. I doubt he can bring himself to admit how he feels to you, but I wouldn't be at all surprised to hear he loves you."

Jill shook her head, needing to ward off the false hope. She couldn't go there. It would lead to more pain in the end.

"I'd like to think so but I can't take that chance. If I married Andrew and it turned out he didn't love me, I wouldn't recover this time, Kel. He would stay with me for the money, but eventually he'd resent me. We'd end up hating each other. Hell, I'd hate myself for keeping him with me. But, I wouldn't be able to let him go."

She swallowed hard, trying to ward off the tears that threatened – but they fell anyway.

Kelly had no more words to offer so she held Jill while she cried. When Jill was spent, Kelly helped her clean up and tucked her into bed before letting herself out the front door.

If Andrew could just stay mad at Jill, he could hold the pain in check. So he worked and he stewed and he stayed angry. He told himself over and over that Jill was just like Blair – that Jill hurt him just like he knew she would.

Over the next two weeks, he threw himself further into work, spending long hours at the office, taking on new projects, and terrorizing his staff with his bitter anger. Andrew knew he was driving everyone around him crazy but he didn't know any other way to keep the pain from bubbling up inside him.

On Thursday afternoon of the second week, Jack finally walked into Andrew's office and shut the door.

"Andrew, you gotta stop this."

"Stop what?" He looked at Jack as if he didn't know what he was talking about but he knew Jack wasn't buying it.

"The whole finance team is walking around on tip-toes because they're afraid of setting you off. I've had three of your staff tell me they need to take their comp time next week. Your staff is trying to get away from you. No one can handle your temper right now."

Andrew let his head fall into his hands. "Yeah, I know. I just really don't know what to do about it."

"What happened with Jill? You told us you broke up but why?"

"I wish I knew. She just said she can't marry me. She's too afraid I'll leave her someday. I gave her a fucking prenup that gave her everything I own if I left her, Jack. What more can I do?"

"Do you love her?" Leave it to Jack to know to ask that question, Andrew thought wryly.

Jack had always been able to read Andrew.

Andrew could only nod.

"Did you tell her that?"

He shook his head. "She's not looking for love. She doesn't believe love can last after what Jake put her through. She wants stability and guarantees, which I gave her, but I guess those aren't enough."

Jack had no answers for Andrew. "Come on. Let's go to my house and let Mrs. Poole spoil us while we get wasted. Kelly's headed to the spa for a long weekend with her sister so we can drown your sorrows in whiskey. I'll have Chad meet us there."

"No, man. I don't want to end up like I did with Blair." Jack and Chad had pulled Andrew out of a week-long drinking binge when Blair left. Andrew had no intention of going down that road again. "I'm just gonna head home."

Jennie knocked on Chad's office door and poked her head in.

"Got a sec, big man?" Jennie asked, irreverent as ever when addressing her boss.

Chad gave her the tolerant sigh he reserved for Jennie and waved her into the room.

She shut the door and took a seat across from his desk.

"So far, I've got nothing we can really document on Theresa. There are odd things. For example, Andrew's been in a piss poor mood the last two weeks since, well you know..."

Chad nodded. He knew Jennie was referring to the tension around the office since Jill and Andrew had called off their engagement.

"Well, the entire finance team is walking around on eggshells. Everyone's miserable. Everyone *except* Theresa. She's been on cloud nine. I found her humming in the copy room today. She's probably ecstatic he split up with Jill."

"Damn. We need something concrete to fire her. 'Gives us the creeps' and 'happy over breakup' are frowned upon in human resources." Chad leaned back in his chair, arms behind his head.

"I could have sworn I saw her coming out of Andrew's office the other day when almost everyone had left for the day. But, it was one of those things where I walked around the corner and she was in front of his office, not in it. It just looked as though she might have just come from there."

Chad sat up. "All right. I'll stay late tonight and put a camera on the door to Andrew's office to log who's entering and when. I don't want to put anything in his office because he holds a lot of meetings with confidential material in there. But one on the door should be okay. I'll let him and Jack know about this."

"I have another idea," Jennie said, but then she hesitated.

He nodded at her expectantly.

"I'd like to log onto her computer and see if I can find anything more incriminating. I don't like the idea of just sitting around waiting to see what she might do if she really is as crazy as I think she is," she said.

He just watched her for a long minute weighing all of their options – the dangers, the pros and cons. Technically, his team or HR were allowed to access any of their employees' computers at any time but it was something they rarely did.

"Let me talk to Jack this weekend and clear it with him. I'll let you know after the weekend if he approves."

"You got it, Herc." Herc was another pet name Jennie reserved just for him. Short for 'Hercules,' it drove him crazy.

He knew that was the allure of the nickname for Jennie. She lived to get a rise out of him.

He glared. "Go."

"Oh, and Jennie," he said as she reached the door to his office, "if we do any snooping on Theresa's computer or desk, we'll do it together. I don't want to take a chance on Theresa catching you alone, peeking through her stuff."

Chad caught Andrew and Jack just as they were leaving.

"Are you serious? Theresa?" Andrew sounded incredulous as he looked from Jack to Chad and back again.

"Jennie was the first one to notice Theresa's odd behavior, but I've seen it since then, too. I'm going to put a camera facing the outside of your door so we can see if she really is going in and out of your office. And, Jack, I want permission to search her desk and computer," Chad said.

"I'll document everything with human resources and get approval as soon as we dot our i's and cross our t's," Jack said, then turned his attention back to Andrew who was still sitting in a chair looking stunned.

"You okay with this?" Jack asked.

"Hmmm? What? Oh, yeah. Fine." His head clearly wasn't on the conversation. Jack threw a quick look to Chad.

"So, Chad'll take care of everything. You just let us know if you see anything unusual going on with Theresa, okay?" Jack asked.

Andrew nodded.

"You okay, Andrew?" Chad asked. "You don't need to worry about this. Jennie and I will take care of Theresa and get her out of here as soon as we can document something that justifies firing her."

Andrew waved off the concerned looks on his friends' faces. "Yeah, sure. I'm just surprised, that's all. Guess I didn't notice anything was going on." He pushed to his feet. "I'm heading out for the rest of the day, guys. I'll see you tomorrow."

He walked out of the office, ignoring the worried looks Chad and Jack exchanged as he left.

CHAPTER 36

Andrew looked around the carriage house and shoved a hand through his hair. It was time for him to pack up and go back to his condo downtown. Lydia and Nora didn't need him here anymore and being so close to Jill was killing him.

Most nights, he couldn't resist watching her as she let Rev out in the backyard to run. He watched from the shadows and stewed and let his anger build.

It was time to put some distance between them. Nora and Lydia had insisted he and Jill would likely work things out before the wedding date. They were plowing ahead with the wedding plans regardless of what he told them.

But that wasn't what he needed. He needed to try to move on and forget that Jill had ever happened.

He shook his head, trying unsuccessfully to clear her from his mind. Thankfully, he hadn't sold the condo. He would pack things up and move back to his place this weekend. He moved to the window and looked down on Jill's yard.

"What the hell?" Andrew said out loud as he watched Jill drive her SUV through her grandparent's backyard, bouncing over the lawn. Jill stopped when she came to the pool, unable to go further.

Reuniting with the Billionaire | 177

He watched as she got out of the truck and ran around the pool. That's when Andrew saw what she was trying to do. Rev was laying on the ground seizing and Jill was struggling to lift him and carry him to her SUV. But eighty pounds of dead weight was clearly more than she could lift for long at a stretch.

"Shit!" he spit the word out as he ran through the door and over to Jill's yard through the woods.

"Jill," he shouted as he came around the back of the fence and jogged toward her.

"He's been seizing for fifteen minutes. I have to get him to the emergency vet." There were tears streaming down her face as she struggled to lift the dog.

"I've got him, honey. I've got him." He lifted Rev and ran to the SUV as Jill followed behind.

"I'll drive. You ride with him," he said as he carefully placed Rev onto the back seat and helped Jill climb in.

Andrew ran around to the front seat and shoved the car in reverse, backing it out of the backyard and onto the driveway.

"Where is the emergency vet?" He asked.

Jill clung to Rev and tried to catch her breath and calm herself.

"On Chase Parkway, near Route 64." She pulled out her cell phone to call and let the vet know she was on her way.

Jill had programmed the number into her phone when Rev was first diagnosed with epilepsy, just in case she ever needed to bring him in after hours for something like this.

Her vet told her if Rev ever seized for longer than five minutes, she needed to take him right in for intravenous anticonvulsants. She was timing carefully. It had already been twenty-two minutes for the seizure by the time Andrew pulled into the vet's parking lot.

Andrew picked up Rev while Jill opened the door to the

clinic. Two technicians met them in the lobby to take them straight back to an exam room.

When they entered the room, Andrew was instructed to put Rev on the table and they began to fire a series of questions about Rev's age, general health, previous seizures and this particular episode.

Within minutes, the doctor entered the room and began to administer medications that would, it was hoped, stop the seizure.

Without looking up, the doctor began to explain what she was doing. "I only have a few more minutes to try to stop this within the thirty-minute window we need to shoot for so I'd like to administer meds and explain later. Do I have your authorization to do that?"

"Yes, that's fine," Jill said. She and her veterinarian had already discussed the danger of a seizure that lasted this long. She knew they needed to stop the seizure before permanent damage was done to his brain.

Rev usually appeared somewhat aware of Jill when he was seizing but now he seemed completely unaware of her and his surroundings. This was worse than anything she'd seen in the past.

The vet tech said his temperature was already at 105. Jill's palms were sweating and she was still shaking from the effort she had exerted trying to get Rev here and the panic she felt when he convulsed.

She watched as the doctor began pushing several medications into the IV and then began to recheck Rev's vital signs. After a few minutes, the doctor turned to Jill and Andrew.

"Hi, I'm Dr. Kerry. Sorry for the late introduction. This is the first time Rev has had a seizure of this length, correct?"

"Yes." Jill nodded as she spoke and put one hand on Rev's leg. She wanted to feel a connection to him and was relieved to feel the tense spasms had left his body already.

"What happened was called status epilepticus. It's essentially any seizure that lasts longer than five minutes. The seizure puts a great deal of strain on the animal's body, which is one of the reasons we saw Rev's temperature shoot up. If we aren't able to stop it quickly, there can be lasting effects, but I think we got to him just in time," Dr. Kerry explained.

"I've given him Diazepam to stop the seizing quickly and Phenobarbital to prevent the seizure starting up again. The Diazepam is fast acting, but it only lasts fifteen to thirty minutes so we need the Phenobarbital on board before the Diazepam wears off."

"Can you tell if there's any permanent damage?" Andrew asked before Jill could and she was glad for his warm strength beside her. She wouldn't have made it here on time if he hadn't come to help.

"At this point we need to wait and see how he responds to the medications. I think, since he's a young, healthy dog and we got to him within the thirty-minute window, he should be fine. I'd like to keep Rev here overnight so we can monitor him and then, if he responds well, you can pick him up tomorrow. You'll need to see your regular veterinarian about getting him on a medication regimen to prevent this from happening again."

"Can we stay with him for a bit?" Jill asked but then winced as she thought that Andrew probably had no interest in staying with her. She should probably offer to take him home, but he nodded at her when she glanced at him.

"Yes. The Phenobarbital is going to keep him under for a while. I had to give him a fairly high dosage so it will have an anesthetic effect for a couple of hours. You can sit with him while we get an overnight suite set up for him. You can come back and visit him early in the morning if you want to but I'd prefer not to release him until tomorrow evening. I want at least twenty-four hours to monitor him."

The doctor and technicians left the room and Jill and Andrew were left alone. She didn't know what to say to Andrew so she pulled a chair closer to where Rev slept and rested her head on him, listening to him breathe.

After what seemed like a very long time, she whispered, "Thank you," to Andrew but couldn't bring herself to look at him.

She wanted to ask how he had been. If he was hurting as much as she'd been hurting for the last two weeks. If he missed her as much as she missed him. If breathing and getting through the day from one minute to the next was as hard for him as it was for her.

He stiffened when she spoke and she held her breath, waiting for a response. She would give anything to be with him, but she couldn't be with him knowing he didn't love her the way she loved him.

"I'll wait outside. Take your time, I have phone calls to make." He stood and walked out of the exam room and Jill wept into Rev's coat.

The fear she had felt during Rev's seizure, combined with the torment of being so close to Andrew but not being able to reach out and have him hold her was more than Jill could handle.

When the vet tech came back twenty minutes later, she had gotten herself somewhat under control but it must have been obvious she'd been crying.

The poor woman tried to assure Jill that Rev was going to be okay now, but that made Jill start crying again. She was relieved Rev would be okay, but Jill knew it would be a long time before she would recover from her broken heart.

CHAPTER 37

Andrew stepped out into the lobby and looked down at his phone. He had said he had phone calls to make but that wasn't true. He just couldn't be in the same room with Jill without pulling her into his arms and holding her.

He knew if he did that, he might break down. His anger at her was slipping away and in its place was a pain so great, he thought it would swallow him whole.

As the anger subsided, he had to admit what he'd known under the surface all along: Jill was nothing like Blair and she would never hurt him the way Blair had.

When Jill left him, she hadn't been motivated by greed or malice. She was just frightened and he couldn't be angry with her for that any longer. It had just been easier for Andrew to hold onto hate and anger instead of feeling the sorrow he felt at losing the woman he loved.

He dropped into a chair in the lobby, his forearms resting on his thighs and his head hanging down. Being close to Jill again was harder than he ever would have imagined.

He wanted to shake her and tell her they belonged together. He imagined if he could tell Jill he loved her, it would all be better. They could go back to the way things should be.

But he knew he couldn't. Not when he knew she couldn't love him back – that she didn't even believe in love. That she wouldn't want to hear those words.

Thirty minutes later, she came down the hall. "I just have to pay the bill and then we can go. They got him moved into the overnight area." She sounded so quiet and sad, it tore at Andrew's heart.

"Okay," was all he could think to say. He clenched his hands by his side to keep from pulling her into his arms and kept himself planted firmly in the seat to keep from going to her.

Twenty minutes later, they were pulling up in front of her front door. He handed her the keys then turned woodenly to walk back to his grandmother's house.

"Andrew."

He took a deep breath to steel himself, then slowly turned to face Jill.

"I need to tell you why I can't marry you. I owe you that much." She looked so sad and alone standing on her front steps. Her arms wrapped around her waist, clinging to herself as if trying to hold herself together.

He watched her, waiting, but didn't say anything. He couldn't breathe. Couldn't move as his senses went on high alert.

She seemed to struggle for a minute before she spoke. "After Jake left, I realized how one-sided things were. How much I had loved Jake... But I honestly don't think he ever loved me. He said he did but it wasn't there. I know that now."

Andrew watched Jill as she blinked back tears and held herself tighter as she talked. He knew every word was costing her. Every word caused her pain and as much as he wanted to hate her, he couldn't. Her pain gutted him.

"I thought I would be okay with the penalty clause, that I would feel secure and know you wouldn't..." Her voice broke and the tears streamed down her face but she continued.

It tore at his heart to see her in such pain... His arms ached to hold her, but he was frozen to the spot. Watching, waiting.

"I fell in love with you, Andrew," she said quietly, tears flowing freely now. "I didn't mean to, but I did and then I realized if we went ahead with the marriage, I would be right back where I started. I would be in a marriage where only one of us was in love and the other was staying for the wrong reasons. I couldn't be with you, knowing you would only be there to avoid losing your money. And I couldn't be married to you knowing you weren't as in love with me as I am with you. I didn't mean to lead you on or make you mad or anything. I'm so sorry. I just... I didn't mean for this to happen."

She bent at the waist, sobbing, as though she couldn't breathe from the pain.

He couldn't move as he processed what Jill said. What it meant for them.

Then he crossed the space to her in two long strides and swept her into his arms. He needed to stop this pain for her. For both of them.

He held on for dear life, holding her tight, understanding then, why he had almost lost her.

"I love you, Jill," he said into her neck. "I've loved you almost since the moment I set eyes on you again. Hell, I don't think I ever stopped loving you as a teenager. I don't know. I just thought if I told you, you'd run like hell. So, I gave you the penalty clause instead."

Andrew felt Jill collapse in his arms and heard her sobs. He pulled back to see her face.

"Don't cry, sweetheart. Why are you still crying?" He wiped the tears from her cheeks with his thumbs and kissed her lips softly.

"I can't help it. I thought...I just...I can't stop crying." She half laughed, half sobbed as she swiped at her tears and smiled a wet smile at him.

"I can fix that," he said. He scooped her up in his arms and carried her in through her front door.

"Say it again," she said.

"I love you. With all my heart. With everything I am. I love you, Jillie Walsh," he whispered and laid kisses on her wet cheeks.

Then her carried her upstairs and showed her how much he loved her again and again, over and over throughout the night. He held her when she slept, spent, in his arms in the early morning light.

CHAPTER 38

*J*ill and Andrew brought Rev home from the hospital the next night and by the following day, he was back to normal. His regular vet put him on a regimen of daily Phenobarbital and they went back to the usual wait-and-see routine with his epilepsy.

As Andrew lay in bed Tuesday morning with Jill snuggled against him, he almost laughed at himself for all the worry he'd held inside.

Telling her he loved her hadn't caused her to turn on him the way it had with Blair. It had set him free. He had never felt more free, more right, more whole at any other time in his life.

She stirred in his arms and he brushed a kiss on her temple.

"Good morning, sweet Jill," he whispered. His gut clenched when she turned her beautiful golden eyes to his.

"Morning, handsome." She stretched her body out, long and lean against his, contorting like a contented cat.

His body instantly came to life and he let his hands trail over her soft, warm skin. Heat flashed between them as Jill turned into his embrace and began the small moaning gasps he loved.

"I love the way your hands feel on me," she said. "The way

they make me feel. I don't think I'll ever get tired of the feel of your hands on me."

Andrew's lips quirked into a smile. "I'll have to keep my hands on you forever, then, sweet Jill. Forever and ever and ever," he said as he added his mouth to his hands.

He still wore that smile when he walked into his office an hour and a half later.

~

Theresa caught the look Andrew gave her as he walked past her desk. He said a quick 'hello' to her that was designed to look like a casual, friendly encounter between two people who worked together to anyone who might be watching, but Theresa knew better.

His lips had quirked at the corners and the look in his eye told her they were more than friends. Or, at least, he wanted them to be more.

On the outside, Andrew looked happy once again now that he and the whore were back together. But Theresa didn't miss the longing looks he snuck her sometimes.

In fact, he'd been watching her more and more lately. She felt his gaze on her whenever he walked down the hall past her desk.

Theresa had been straightening Andrew's office for him one evening and found the prenuptial agreement the whore had forced him to sign. That was all the proof she needed to know he was in trouble.

She didn't know yet what hold this woman had on him but it must be strong if she had manipulated Andrew into signing away all of his wealth to her.

Maybe his little tramp had something she was holding over him.

That wouldn't last long. Theresa would find out what the hell was going on and fix it for Andrew. And, when he finally got out from under the bitch's spell, she would be there for him. To help him pick up the pieces. To answer those silent pleas he'd had been sending Theresa all this time.

CHAPTER 39

Jill was surprised to hear the doorbell ring. She rarely had visitors at the house and wasn't expecting anyone. Andrew would be home soon, but he never rang the bell.

Jake. Great. Just great. Jill stepped away from the window and opened the front door.

"What can I do for you, Jake?" It wasn't a stretch for her to add a touch of annoyance to her voice and she hoped it would eventually discourage his surprise visits.

He smiled and pulled a bouquet of carnations from behind his back.

Really? Carnations? Is there any cheesier flower than that?

He seemed to be waiting for a response. She had no intention of inviting him inside so she stepped out onto the front porch, taking the carnations as she walked. She leaned against the porch railing and set the flowers next to her.

"Jake, what's this about? Why do you keep doing this?" She tilted her head and studied the man she had once loved. The man who'd walked away from her.

"I miss you, Jill. I've been thinking and I think I made a big mistake. I want us to try again."

"What!" she sputtered. "I... That's insane... I don't even know what to say to that."

He took her hand but she pulled it back from him.

"Please, Jill. Say you'll give us another try. I broke things off with Missy. I know I was wrong, but I can do this. I can make this work. I know I can." He sounded earnest, but there were an awful lot of 'I's in what he'd said.

She shook her head. "I'm not some project for you to keep working at."

"I know, Jill. But we're good together. We had such a good life, together, you know?"

"No. I don't know. I've realized a lot of things over the past several months. Our marriage wasn't right, Jake. I thought I was happy, but I didn't see how much I was giving up. I'm sorry, but I don't love you anymore." Jill tried to be calm and firm, wondering if maybe this time he'd listen to her. For once, would he just listen?

"But Jill," he began.

"No. Stop." She sighed. "Look, Jake. I'm sorry, but I'm not going to give us another try. I'm in love with someone else. I'm getting married to a man I love with all my heart. And the best part is, he loves me just as much. He respects me. He would never treat me the way you treated me."

His face grew hard and his hands gripped her arms tightly. Too tightly.

"You can't. You can't marry someone else. You're supposed to love *me*, Jill." Jake's eyes were hard and flashed with anger.

She didn't know if she was more stunned that he had grabbed her or that he *still* didn't care about her feelings. How had she not seen him for who he truly was over the time they'd been together?

She didn't have much time to respond to him because Jake was lifted off the ground and tossed down the porch stairs.

"Oh, God, Andrew. Don't hurt him!" Jill grabbed Andrew's arm and tried to pull him back.

She'd have better luck stopping a freight train, but it only took Andrew a few seconds to get himself under control.

"Leave. Now," he bit out through clenched teeth.

Jake scrambled backwards in the driveway as Andrew stalked him.

When his feet finally found purchase, Jake scurried to his car and quickly drove away while Jill pulled Andrew back to the porch.

Her arms tingled as Andrew ran his hands gently over them, scowling at the red blotches that were blossoming on her arm where Jake had grabbed her. He let out a deep roar and turned back toward his car, presumably to go after Jake, but she grabbed his arm and pulled him back to the porch.

"It's not important, Andrew. Let him go."

"Did he hurt you?" His voice rippled with anger. He was controlling it, but only just.

"I'm okay. He wouldn't have really hurt me," she answered.

She slipped her hands around Andrew's back and brushed her hands up and down in long strokes, soothing away the tension.

"What did he want?"

"Nothing. It's not important." She turned and opened the door to let out a frantic Rev. "It's all right. Mommy's fine." Jill knelt down to scratch Rev and reassure him. When she stood back up, she ran into the brick wall of Andrew's chest.

His arms came back up to her shoulders, pinning her firmly, but gently. His eyes pierced hers in a steady gaze.

"What did he want, Jill?" He said every word slowly, carefully.

"It was silly. It's nothing." She shrugged a shoulder. "He's apparently tired of Missy and wants to get back together with me. Obviously I told him that wasn't going to happen and he didn't like that answer."

Andrew was still for a minute and then bent to look into Jill's eyes. His voice was soft and quiet when he finally spoke. "Do you want that, Jill? You were with him a long time. Are you sure you don't need to see where that might go?"

She took a step back and studied Andrew's face to be sure he was serious. He looked deadly serious and the realization made her a little sick.

"How could you even think that?" She shook her head at him. "How could that even cross your mind? There isn't anything Jake could say or do to make me want to be back with him." She studied his face again to see if he understood. "*You*. You're my world, Andrew. What you and I have together is so different, so much more than anything Jake and I ever shared. I wouldn't give up what you and I have – for Jake or anyone else."

His smile was slow, sexy, the kind of smile that burned through Jill and heated her from the inside out. With that one smile, he changed the air between them. Suddenly there was a crackling heat that charged between their bodies. He called Rev inside and pulled Jill into the house behind him.

Her arms wound their way around his neck and her body pressed into his as if it had a mind of its own. Every fiber of her wanted to be closer to Andrew, wanted to feel him pressed against her.

His hands went around her bottom and he scooped her up, pulling her tight to him as his mouth devoured hers with a heated kiss.

She wrapped her legs around his waist and matched the heat in his kiss with passion of her own. She felt her nipples pebble against his chest and let the friction of their joined bodies thrill through her.

"Dining room," Jill said, her lips still on his.

A small chuckle came from deep in his chest as he lay her on the dining room table and began to work the button on her jeans.

Jill tugged at Andrew's shirt, trying to pull it free of his jeans, wanting to touch his muscled chest. He paused and pulled his shirt over his head with one arm and then made quick work of the rest of their clothes.

"God, what you do to me," he murmured to her as he entered her slowly, plunging deep and then staying as still as he could as if trying to gain some semblance of control.

She laughed but it was thready and needy and her nails dug into his hips, urging him to move within her. Regaining control, he moved slowly, drawing a tortured moan from her.

"Mine." Andrew's voice was raspy, husky with desire and possession as he brought Jill closer and closer to orgasm.

"Only yours," Jill whispered.

Slowly, deeply, he plunged harder, drawing gasp after gasp from her until she shattered beneath him, spinning blissfully out of control.

And, somehow, when she returned to earth, she found him smiling at her, still in control, ready for more.

"Put your arms around my neck and hold on, sweetheart," Andrew whispered, his voice ragged.

She held on while he lifted her and carried her to the couch where he sat, still inside Jill as she straddled him. He gave her free rein now, letting her loose to set her own pace on top of him.

When their bodies were entwined together, the hard, slick heat of him filling her so completely, she lost all control.

She wanted him deeper, faster, harder and with Andrew, Jill took what she wanted. She bent her head and nipped at his neck, writhing, engulfed in sensation as she rocked her hips into him over and over. She exploded in pleasure once again, bringing him with her as she went.

Theresa's hands gripped the steering wheel so tightly, her knuckles turned white. She was stunned as she sat outside Jill's house and watched Andrew chase off the man Jill had been whoring around with.

My God, Andrew catches her in the act, with another man on her front steps, and still, he doesn't see her for what she is! This has to stop.

She had assumed Andrew was being pushed into this by his family, but maybe she was wrong. Maybe he was really taken in by this manipulative bitch.

Theresa took deep breaths as she slowly, carefully pulled the car away from the curb. The calm, deliberate movements soothed her.

Breathe in. Breathe out.

CHAPTER 40

Christmas that year was by far the best holiday Jill had ever had. She and Andrew traveled to her parents' house for the holiday and spent almost a week with them.

He hit it off with her parents immediately. They had met Andrew in the past, of course, but hadn't seen him in years. She was happy to see her parents really liked Andrew.

He spent time with her dad in the garage playing around with a car he was restoring. She and her mom looked through wedding magazines and Jill was relieved that this visit had come after she and Andrew had acknowledged they loved one another. The thought of facing her parents had seemed daunting when her wedding was more about a contract between two good friends than love.

With Andrew's love and support behind her, she was happy to bury herself in wedding plans and hopes for future babies.

Andrew surprised Jill on Christmas morning with an antique box camera he'd found on Etsy. It was by far the most thoughtful present she'd ever received. For his gift, she had printed several of the shots she'd captured during their trip to Big Bend and had them framed for Andrew's office.

Now, she and Andrew sat on the back swing on her parents'

porch. They snuggled together with mugs of mulled wine to keep their hands warm and rocked lazily in the crisp evening air.

Jill felt completely at peace. Content. It was hard to believe she had felt so off-kilter just a few months earlier, as if her whole world had been rocked and she would never find her axis again.

Now, she knew that Andrew *was* her axis. Her whole world hadn't truly ever been in balance before him.

She let out a soft mewl of happiness as she let her hand play up and down his stomach, to his chest and back down again. The feel of his strong arms around her and his warm body pressed against hers had Jill almost dozing off to sleep as they rocked.

"I think I want six." Andrew really wanted four kids, but he figured he'd start the conversation at six so Jill would have some room to talk him down.

"Hmm? Six what?" she asked. She didn't raise her head from his side.

"Six kids." Now Jill's head came up. "Six! Are you crazy? I'm thirty-five years old, Andrew. When do you think I'm going to pop out these six babies?"

Andrew laughed. "Five?" He countered.

"Two."

"Four and a half?"

"Half?"

"Well, that's how you negotiate," Andrew explained. "I gotta have something left to throw away after you make your next bid."

She shook her head but he could see the laughter in her eyes.

"Three. That's it, mister. Three." Jill laid her head back down on Andrew's chest.

He waited a few beats, letting the swing soothe her back to her lazy, relaxed state.

"Okay. Four," he said quietly.

He felt her soft laugh against his chest and pulled her tighter, kicking his legs to keep the slow rhythm of the swing going.

CHAPTER 41

Chad had walked past Jennie's desk at noon the first day back at work after Christmas. He paused and leaned down so that only Jennie would hear his words.

"Stay late tonight? We got the go ahead from Jack and Human Resources."

She nodded at him and he kept walking.

She met Chad in his office at the end of the day, knocking once and opening the door to his answering grunt.

"Hey," she said, tugging the door shut behind her. "Theresa just left. There are a few people left on the other side of the building but everyone over here has left for the day. If you keep watch while I go through her desk, we should be okay."

Chad didn't say anything. He just shut down his computer and stood up, waiting for Jennie to go back through the door to the outer offices.

She walked over to Theresa's desk while Chad placed himself in a spot that let him see down the hallway to the rest of the offices but also allowed him to watch Jennie. She quickly began opening desk drawers.

"Did you get her computer password in case we need it?" Jennie asked quietly. Everyone had their computers password protected, but the tech department kept the passwords on file and all employees knew their computers could be accessed by the company without notice.

Chad grimaced. "TWESTON."

It took Jennie a minute to process that. *Ugh. Not good.* That alone would probably be going into the file as part of their justification for letting her go.

The third drawer Jennie opened got them what they needed. A folder sat underneath the intra-company phone directory. Jennie opened it to scan the contents and gave Chad a nod.

She shut the drawer, file in hand, and both she and Chad slipped back into his office. She spread out the contents of the folder on his desk.

There were several printouts of email messages that supposedly showed communications from Jill to Kelly. The emails showed Jill bragging about getting Andrew to sign a prenuptial agreement, then detailed information about Andrew's accounts and property he owned.

"This isn't Kelly's email address and I'm willing to bet this isn't Jill's either," Jennie said.

Chad flipped through the pages of emails. There was an invoice from a private investigator. The invoice was written to Jill Walsh and charged $550 for investigative work regarding Andrew Weston's personal financial records.

There were several newspaper clippings that mentioned or featured Andrew. They dated back as far as a year.

The last item in the folder was a prenuptial agreement between Jill and Andrew. Chad flipped through to the final page of the contract and read the signatures.

"This looks real. It's Andrew's signature, at least. He also told me about the prenup," he said.

"Then she probably *had* just come out of Andrew's office when I saw her that day. This other stuff all looks fake. She's setting Jill up, I'd guess. Trying to make it look like Jill is after Andrew's money?"

"I'll see if Andrew and Jill can meet us over at Jack's," Chad said.

∼

Jack and Kelly's housekeeper, Mrs. Poole greeted Chad with a warm hug and then showed Jennie and Chad into the living room, where Jack, Kelly, Andrew, and Jill waited.

"I'll have dinner ready in about thirty minutes," Mrs. Poole said before leaving the room. She obviously loved to mother everyone whenever she had the chance.

Chad handed Andrew the folder Jennie had found and Andrew and Jill sat side by side flipping through the contents. Jill gasped when she saw the emails in the folder, but before she could speak, Andrew did.

"The emails are fakes," Andrew said. "I'm guessing the invoice from the private investigator is fake, too. Jill didn't hire him, but it's possible Theresa posed as her and hired him. That or it's just a forgery. It'd be easy enough to create a fake invoice. The newspaper articles and the prenuptial agreement are real. The prenup was filed in my office."

Jill smiled up at him, warmth obvious in her gaze at the realization that he hadn't questioned the veracity of the materials for even a second. There wasn't a shred of doubt about her loyalty to him anywhere in his voice. There wasn't a hint of question in his eyes when he leaned in and kissed her gently.

Jennie's heart felt battered and bruised whenever she was near Jack and Kelly and now she could add Jill and Andrew to that list. She didn't begrudge them their happiness at all, but it didn't make her pain any less in the face of that kind of devotion.

"I called Jarrod and asked him to meet us here. He should be here soon," Chad said as Andrew passed the folder over so Jack could look through.

Jarrod Harmon was a friend of Chad's on the police force.

Chad went on. "This gives us all we need to fire Theresa, but I think this also goes farther. When we found this, I had to wonder if Theresa might have had something to do with Debbie's mysterious mugging and Patty's hit-and-run."

"Oh, My God, do you really think she'd do that?" Jill asked.

"I've seen the way she watches Andrew," Jennie said. "And I saw the way she looked at you at the holiday party. If given the chance, I think she would have torn you apart, Jill. It was scary."

Before Jill could answer, Mrs. Poole showed Jarrod into the living room. The tall, lean man's face looked grim and he didn't stop for niceties.

"I ran a little check on Theresa Sawyer and her car matches the description of the car that hit your employee last month. I was also able to look a little further back in her record than your typical employee background check goes. It was a long time ago, but she does have some charges against her. There were a couple of trespassing charges and a breaking and entering charge. Those are often the kind of thing we see on the records of stalkers."

Andrew handed Jarrod the folder with what they'd just uncovered and went through what was real and what was fake.

Jarrod flipped through the materials, scanning quickly. His eyebrows went up and he looked at Andrew. "You signed this?" Jarrod asked, indicating the prenup.

Andrew laughed and Jill's cheeks flushed. Jarrod was looking at the page with the penalty clause.

"It was a tactical decision," Andrew said with a squeeze of Jill's hand.

"Remind me never to hire you to negotiate for me," Jarrod said while the others laughed.

The group sobered as Jarrod shut the folder and brought them back around to the business at hand.

"Based on this, the make and model of Theresa's car, and the connection of the victims to Andrew and Theresa, I'm going to see if I can get a warrant to search Theresa's home. I'm not sure it will be enough, but I'll see what I can do. I'll call you guys as soon as I know anything," Jarrod said.

Dinner was a little quieter than it normally was with so many friends at the table. Kelly and Jennie worked to keep up chatter about wedding dresses, cakes, and caterers but there was a layer of tension beneath the surface that everyone seemed to feel.

As they helped Mrs. Poole clear away the plates and cleanup, Chad's phone rang. He left the room to talk for a few minutes, before returning to report to the group.

"Jarrod convinced a judge to give him a search warrant," Chad reported. "Theresa wasn't around when they executed it. They found a knife that might match the knife used on Debbie and it has some trace blood on it. It'll take a long time to process through the lab, though. They're hoping to find her car so they can test for blood on the bumper but so far, Theresa hasn't turned up."

"Anything else?" Andrew asked as he wrapped his arms around Jill in a protective shell.

"Uh. Yeah." Chad looked uncomfortable as he glanced at Jill before continuing. "They found a lot of stuff about Andrew. Newspaper clippings. Pictures. Some from around the office and some taken around your condo. A few pictures of you at Nora's house. There are pictures of Jill, too. A journal with a whole bunch of bizarre ramblings. Uh, stuff about you and Theresa being made for each other, signs you send to her to let her know you love her even though you have to be with Jill. Weird shit."

Andrew was quiet for a minute.

"I think we should get out of here for the weekend," he said. "We can go up to the cabin. If the police haven't found Theresa by Monday, we can figure something else out, but let's just get out of harm's way for the weekend?"

"I'll go up with you. Jack and Kelly, work for you guys?" Chad asked as he looked around the room to nods and murmurs of agreement.

After making plans to leave the following morning, Jill and Andrew returned to her house for a tense night that provided very little sleep.

CHAPTER 42

Theresa seethed as she let her car roll to a stop outside her office building. She'd spotted the police in her apartment last night when she got home and was able to sneak back to her car and leave before they saw her.

She wasn't sure yet if it would be safe for her to go to work, but her doubts were confirmed when she saw the police car in front of the building.

That fucking slut. What did Andrew's little whore do now? This had to be linked to her. Andrew would never betray me. Our love is too strong for that. This could only be his fucking whore at work.

Theresa drove around to the back of the building and entered the parking garage. She drove past Andrew's reserved parking spot.

Empty.

So were the spots reserved for Chad Thompson and Jack Sutton. *The cabin.* They must have all gone up to the ski cabin together.

Well, I'll just go to the ski house, too.

It was time to take care of the fiancée, Theresa's way. No more waiting for Andrew to see the bitch for what she was.

For all his wonderful qualities, Theresa had to admit, Andrew was a bit weak when it came to whatever hold his little whore had on him. He was weak and blind and, apparently, unable to act on his own. But that was all right.

That's what Andrew had Theresa for. It was why they were so good together. They complemented one another so well. What Andrew couldn't bring himself to do, Theresa could. For Andrew, she could do it. She would take care of the damn whore.

∽

Missy listened to Jake's voice through the phone but had a hard time believing what he said.

How could he do this to me after what we've shared? I just don't understand this.

"You can't mean that, Jake," she said, pleading with him again.

"I do mean it, Missy. It's over. I'm working on getting my marriage back on track. I'm getting back together with Jill," came his answer.

"But, you divorced her. It's not like it was just a separation. The divorce is final. You divorced her for me. For us. So we could be together."

"I'm sorry, Missy. I made a mistake. You need to understand that. I can't be with you anymore."

Missy heard the line go dead and knew Jake had hung up. She just stared at the phone. This conversation hadn't gone any differently than the last ten times she had called him over the past few weeks.

She tried to go on without him and she would do well for a few days, but then she lost her resolve and called again. She knew she needed to keep trying. She had to think about her baby. Their baby.

He had broken things off with her as soon as he found out she was pregnant. She'd been stunned. Numb for weeks.

Was it really possible he could be so cruel? So brutally cold as to leave her and try to work things out with his ex-wife just when she found out she was pregnant with his child? How had she miscalculated so severely? How could she have been so wrong about the kind of person he was? About his love for her?

She slipped her phone in her pocket. She would go talk to Jill. If she told Jill about the baby and asked her to step aside, to let Missy and Jake be together for the sake of their baby, maybe she could convince him to come back to her. To his family.

She drove almost blindly to the address she had for Jill. She had seen the directions written on a notepad in Jake's office one day. When she asked why he had Jill's new address, he'd told her he had to take over some paperwork related to the divorce. Now she wondered if he'd been visiting Jill all along.

Missy parked a block away and walked over. She needed to gather her courage to do this.

Jill would see her as a homewrecker. As the mistress. But that wasn't what Missy was. Not really.

She had never intended to fall for Jake. He was just so convincing. Before she knew it, she had fallen in love and there wasn't any turning back.

But turn back was what Missy wanted to do now. She wanted to run away, but she needed to do this. She stood across from Jill's house, hands in her pockets watching, thinking, trying to muster up the courage to walk up the driveway and ask Jill to let go of the man she loved.

CHAPTER 43

Andrew and Jill arrived minutes behind Chad, Jennie, Jack, and Kelly. He could tell Jill was worried. Neither of them had slept well the night before and the strain around the corner of Jill's mouth was clear anytime he looked her way.

She was tense and had barely commented on any of the scenery during the drive. She would normally spot any wildlife and point out pretty trees or even rows of houses that were somehow unique or eye catching.

They needed the respite the cabin offered. They piled out of their cars and began to unload luggage and dogs.

Jill let Rev out of his crate in the back of Jill's SUV and Jennie sprang Zeke and Zoe from their crates in the back of Jack's vehicle. They all laughed as the dogs raced in circles, burning off energy after the long road trip.

As he always did, Chad took Jennie's bag along with his and carried it into the house. Andrew shook his head. That man was in love with Jennie.

After everyone settled into their rooms, Chad, Jennie, Jack, and Kelly decided to get in a half-day of skiing.

Andrew pulled Jill onto his arms. "We'll stay here and snuggle. I'm beat."

Jack and Chad gave him equally lecherous smiles. "Sure, you stay here and rest," Jack said and the others walked out the door.

In all honesty, Andrew was exhausted. He had spent half the night awake. Worrying. Watching Jill sleep. Wondering how he would survive if anything happened to her. Jarrod texted this morning to let him know that Theresa hadn't shown up for work today. She was now officially in the wind.

Andrew was pretty sure Theresa didn't know about the ski cabin but he didn't want to chance leaving Jill there alone while he went skiing. He knew she would normally go out on her snowshoes and look for wildlife to photograph, but he hoped he could keep her inside.

They settled on the couch in front of the fire, her soft, warm body wrapped up in his. She fit in his arms in a way no one else had. Andrew tucked Jill's head under his chin and held her tight.

"You okay?" She was idly tracing a path up his arm and back down with her fingers, the soft rhythm of it almost putting Andrew into a trance.

"Hmm. Just tired. I'll be glad when this is over so I can relax."

She continued the soothing stroke up and down his arms as, despite his best intentions, he fell asleep in front of the fire.

Jill heard Andrew's breathing become soft and steady – the steady breathing of sleep. She carefully lifted his arm off of her stomach and slid out from under him. Ouch! Her legs had gone to sleep and Jill gritted her teeth as the pins and needles hit.

Shaking her legs out, she wandered to the kitchen to see what supplies were left from the last trip. They always had plenty of canned goods on hand and there was beer and wine in the fridge. Nothing fresh, though. They should have stopped on the way to stock up on food for the weekend.

Looking at Andrew asleep on the couch, she debated going to

get groceries. Even though they didn't think Theresa knew about the cabin, Jill figured it was better to wait for Andrew to wake up so they could go together.

She sat down and read a few chapters of a book and then worked for a bit on her laptop, cataloguing pictures for her website. An hour into the work, she was interrupted by the quiet buzz of Andrew's phone vibrating on the kitchen counter. Jill picked it up and looked at the display: Jarrod Harmon.

"Hi Jarrod," Jill whispered into the phone. "Andrew's asleep. It's Jill."

"Hi, Jill. Just wanted to let you know we got Theresa. She was standing outside your house, actually. Staring at the house. They haven't found her car yet, and she's not talking. No ID on her, but she matches the description: five feet, four inches, brown hair, brown eyes. I'll confirm ID for sure when I get down to the station but you guys can breathe easier."

"Oh, that's great, Jarrod. Andrew was up all night worrying and he won't let me out of his sight. I'll let him know as soon as he wakes up. Do you need us to come back before Monday for anything?" she asked, feeling a weight lift from her chest.

"Nah. You guys are fine. I'll handle things from this end and get statements from you all on Monday. Tell Andrew to take it easy."

"Thank you, Jarrod," she said and cut the connection.

She blew out a breath and looked at Andrew. He was still out cold, stretched along the length of the couch. After letting her eyes roam over his body for a few minutes, she smiled and turned back to the kitchen.

She hadn't been sure Theresa would do much more than yell at her or something if she came to confront her, but still, she could feel the difference in the set of her shoulders now the tension had left her.

"Might as well go get groceries," she whispered to the dogs.

Rev and Zoe began wagging their tails furiously while she scribbled a note to Andrew.

"Uh uh. You guys wait here. I'll take you out for a hike when I get back."

She grabbed her purse and slipped out the door, shutting it behind her before the dogs could follow.

There hadn't been fresh snow for a few days on the mountain. Although the land around the cabin was still covered in snow, the road was mostly clear. There were a few patchy ice spots, so Jill guided her SUV carefully down the steep road.

She slowed when she approached the Gunderson's driveway. It was a long drive that was covered in heavy woods near the end. Because of the trees it was impossible to see if a car was about to turn onto the road, so they'd all gotten used to slowing there to be sure.

After she passed the driveway, she saw a small sedan turn onto the road behind her. Although she didn't recognize the sedan as one of the Gunderson's cars, Jill didn't think anything of the other driver's presence until she saw the car suddenly speed toward her in the rear-view mirror.

Her stomach lurched at the sight.

Oh, no! They must be hydroplaning.

It seemed the only explanation for such a sudden burst of speed on an icy road. Then the sedan clipped the rear bumper of Jill's explorer. Not enough to cause a major accident, but just enough to send Jill sliding a bit.

She quickly got control of her vehicle and pulled to a stop. She didn't want to end up in the shoulder where there was still soft snow. She'd have trouble getting out of there, so she just nosed her SUV to a halt on the very edge of the road.

The sedan skidded a bit but stopped. Jill saw the driver coming toward her and rolled down the window to let the driver know she was safe. The last thing she saw before her world went black was the large rock in the driver's hand.

Puzzled as to why the driver would be holding a rock, Jill didn't even process the fact that the rock was being swung with great force at her head until it was too late.

She raised her arms and tried to fight the woman off, but that hesitation had cost her. Too much.

CHAPTER 44

Well, that was easy. I'm really getting good at this.

Theresa had taken some confidence-boosting courses online and knew it was important to recognize her own self-worth and affirm her value routinely. She opened the door to Jill's car and dragged the unconscious woman from the vehicle.

Jill's body fell to the ground with a thud.

Thank God for deserted mountain roads, huh?

Theresa laughed as she hauled Jill up by the arms and dragged her to the back door of her sedan. After shoving Jill into the backseat of the car, Theresa hopped back in the driver's seat and proceeded down the mountain, humming as she drove.

I wonder what song that is? Oh well. Doesn't matter.

Theresa hummed her unknown tune for twenty minutes as she drove off the mountain and toward major highways where she could put some distance between her car and anyone who might come looking for the little whore.

When she hit the highway, she spoke to Jill, who lay in the backseat, bleeding from a head wound.

"Time for you to pay for your little plot against my Andrew, slut." Theresa looked in the rearview mirror as she spoke to her passenger, as if she were speaking to a willing passenger instead of an unconscious person lying prone along the backseat. Her tone was calm and conversational. "You and I are going to find a quiet place together, where we can have a chat. I'll get you to admit everything you've done to Andrew. All your conniving manipulation."

Theresa patted the video camera sitting on the seat next to her.

"And when I tape your confession and show my Andrew what you truly are, what a fucking performer you are, with all your twisted dishonesty laid out for him, there won't be any more barriers between Andrew and me."

At that point, an acerbic, petulant tone had crept into Theresa's speech. It was probably the distraction of her ranting at Jill that caused Theresa's foot to lay too heavily on the gas pedal as she flew down the highway.

The burst of red and blue lights behind her came as a complete surprise. When she heard the siren, Theresa pulled to the side of the road and schooled her face into one of innocence and concern.

Theresa remained calm as she watched the officer walk up to her window. She decided a good offense was better than being defensive and rolled the window down.

"Officer, Thank God. I don't know where the hospital is. I've looked for signs but I don't know where I'm going," Theresa cried out in her best help-me-I'm-just-a-poor-helpless-female voice.

The officer peered into the backseat at Jill, though he stood several feet back from the vehicle, one hand on his gun belt as if poised to make a stand.

Fool.

"My friend was in an accident and hit her head. I'm trying to get her to a hospital."

The officer appeared to assess Theresa, then made a decision.

"Follow me. The hospital is two exits ahead," he said and turned back to his car.

Theresa was no idiot. She knew the officer would have called in the stop and she knew if she didn't follow him now, he would chase her down and she'd really have a problem on her hands.

Not a problem. I can adapt. It's important to be able to handle change.

She smiled and gave herself a mental high five. She was really proud of the way she was handling all of this. Someday, Andrew would be proud, too, when she told him everything she'd had to do to pull her plan together.

When the emergency room personnel wheeled her 'friend' in on a gurney, a nurse turned to Theresa and asked if her friend had any identification on her.

"Oh, no. I left her purse in her car. I didn't even think to grab it when she ran off the road. I'm sorry. Her name is Christina. Christina Robins." Theresa offered the name of her nosy next-door neighbor with the smelly cat. That damned animal was always trying to slip into Theresa's apartment whenever she opened the door.

"We're going to get your friend set up for a CT Scan and run some tests. We'll let you know as soon as you can see her."

Theresa smiled. "I can wait," she said sweetly to the nurse.

"Is there family in the area you can call for her? Anyone you can alert?" the helpful nurse asked.

"No. There's no one to call. I'm all she has now," Theresa said with a small shake of her head.

She sat down to wait and formulate a new plan.

CHAPTER 45

*A*ndrew wasn't sure how long he slept. He woke with a start and looked around. He could tell almost immediately Jill wasn't in the cabin. Icy fingers of dread crept up his spine but he swept them aside. Nothing could go wrong up here and him jumping at every little thing wouldn't do them any good.

Jill had probably gone out on her snowshoes or was sitting outside on the deck. He sat up but realized the dogs were inside with him.

That means she's not outside. Why the fuck did I fall asleep?

He rubbed his face with his hands to wake himself up and then walked to the front of the cabin and looked out.

The car was gone. Looking at his watch, he saw that it was only two o'clock. He had probably only been asleep about an hour or so. She couldn't be far.

He dialed Jill's phone but it went to voicemail and needling doubts worked their way in again.

"Hey, hon. Just woke up. Wanted to know where you are. Call me when you get this... I love you."

He knew he shouldn't be panicking, but anxiety swamped his brain. What if Theresa followed them up here? What if they were wrong and Theresa did know about the ski house?

He couldn't handle it if anything happened to Jill. He'd only just found her after being alone for so long. What would he do if he lost her?

Even the idea of it made his stomach clench and his heart beat out a too fast rhythm in his chest. But he was overreacting and he told himself that.

But when he tried to tell himself to calm down, he remembered that the police had every reason to believe Theresa had hurt other people close to him. Debbie and Pat, who had only gotten in her way at work. What would she do to his fiancée?

Andrew walked into the kitchen and saw some of the cabinet doors were open. A wave of relief hit him hard when he saw Jill's note.

'Jarrod called. They have Theresa! Went to store for groceries. Be back soon.'

He stood and gripped the counter, head hanging as he sucked in a deep breath, then another. She was okay. He'd been worried for nothing.

He went back to the living room and let the dogs out for a run in the yard taking another deep breath as relief washed through him. It was over. Theresa hadn't hurt Jill.

He watched the dogs play for a few minutes, then called them back into the house. Moments later, his phone rang. He checked call display.

"Hey, Jarrod, what's up?"

"I'm sorry, Andrew. I told Jill we had Theresa in custody. I have bad news. It wasn't Theresa they picked up. We thought it was because the lady they found was standing with no ID outside Jill's house – just watching the house. She was sure as hell acting like a stalker and she fit the physical description to a 'T.' When we finally got her to stop crying and talk to us, it turns out she's been dating Jill's ex but he dumped her. She just wanted to talk to Jill."

Andrew's whole body froze as he listened. Jill was out there alone and so was Theresa. The familiar feelings of dread came back in waves, this time hitting harder than ever.

"I gotta go, Jarrod. Jill went out alone. I have to find her."

Andrew didn't wait for an answer. He ran back into the house to grab his car keys, then realized he didn't have a car. Jill had her car and the others had taken Jack's car to the ski resort. As Andrew looked around wondering about the sanity of taking one of the snowmobiles all the way into town to the grocery store, his phone rang.

Chad.

"Chad, you guys need to get back here. I need the car to go after Jill," he said without preamble.

"Come down the hill, Andrew. Grab one of the snowmobiles. Kelly was feeling sick so we called it quits early. We were on our way back up. Jill's car is stopped on the road, but she's nowhere in sight."

Icy fear twisted around his lungs, his heart. Andrew couldn't breathe, couldn't move for a split second. A rush of terror coursed through his veins and he began to react.

He grabbed the snowmobile keys from the hook on the wall and dashed outside. All he could think was that he needed to get to Jill.

But he wouldn't be able to. She was gone.

It didn't take him long to get to where her SUV sat abandoned. His friends were already calling out Jill's name as if hoping she might be nearby.

They had split up and headed in different directions, calling and searching for Jill.

Chad approached Andrew.

"Her purse is in the car. There's a small dent and some paint transfer on the back bumper. We've called Jason Graham. He's on his way."

Jason was the fire chief and also a good friend. Andrew knew he'd move mountains to help them find Jill.

He stared at Jill's empty car and felt sick to his stomach. Kelly came up behind him and wrapped her arms around his waist and hugged.

"They thought they had Theresa." Andrew could hear how thick his voice sounded. He didn't even recognize his own voice, it was so laden with fear. "Jarrod called and told Jill Theresa was in custody, but that was a mistake."

"Hey, we'll find her," Kelly said fiercely. "Jason's on his way. You guys tracked me when I was gone. We'll find Jill."

Jason pulled up in a truck with several other people and a large shepherd-looking dog. Jason made introductions, but Andrew couldn't process anyone's name.

The men discussed several possible scenarios: Jill walking away from the car for some reason; someone driving her away from the car; Jill being thrown from the vehicle. The last was dismissed. There was no evidence of the type of crash that could have caused that and her windshield was intact.

While two men began to search the tree line along the road, Andrew watched as the dog was shown the driver's side of Jill's car. The dog sniffed at the seat for several seconds and was then given a quiet command by his handler.

Dog and handler began to circle the car then walked about six feet from the car and stopped. The handler took the dog back to the car and the dog repeated the same sequence, going six feet in exactly the same direction and stopping at the same point. This was repeated a third time.

The handler bent to the ground where the dog stopped and then both handler and dog jogged over to Andrew and Jason. Andrew felt the blow deep in his gut as the handler spoke.

"Justice began working a track from the driver's side but then stops. It's as if the track ends in the middle of the road. There are some spots in the road. A small patch of what might be oil. It's possible a car was stopped in the road at the spot where Justice stopped tracking. There are plenty of footprints there and also a few drops of what could be blood. Crime scene won't be here for another thirty minutes to confirm," the man reported to Jason.

The handler seemed reticent to draw any conclusions, which Andrew could understand. But, he wasn't an idiot. Andrew knew Jill was likely put in a car and driven away.

"Kelly, any luck?" Andrew called to where Kelly was making phone calls.

"Nothing. No Jill Walshes or Jane Does in any hospitals nearby," Kelly reported.

"We've got an all points out on Jill. Someone will spot her, Andrew," Jason said.

"Jason, you've known me for six years. I can't just stand around and wait. That's not gonna happen," Andrew said.

Chad and Jack closed in around Andrew, waiting for directions, their silent support indicating they understood the need to do something instead of sitting on a fucking mountain to wait.

Hell, even if they hadn't understood, they would stand by Andrew's decision.

Chad spoke next. "Jason, how sure are they that she didn't walk away from the car or that someone didn't take her into the woods here?"

"There's no evidence of anyone walking into the woods. With the level of snow we still have on the ground, we would see any disturbance clearly. Justice is an extremely capable dog with an experienced handler. He can't tell us for sure what happened, but I think Jill got into a car." As Jason finished his assessment, Kelly walked up.

"I've called the Gundersons and the Peters. Jill isn't at either of their houses and they haven't seen anything unusual in the area."

The Gundersons and the Peters were the only other families on the mountain.

"If Jill's been taken off the mountain, then we need to leave the mountain," Andrew said.

He could see Jason struggling with his response. It probably was not at all normal for the fire chief to leave the scene and go looking for a missing person with the missing person's friends. Most likely Jason was risking his job to go with them.

The man rubbed his hand over the back of his neck and let out a frustrated groan. "Fuck it. I'll drive."

∽

Jill's head was pounding and her eyes wouldn't open. She moved her head but was immediately rewarded with searing pain that brought on a wave of nausea.

She heard a whimper and thought it might have come from her. Then a soft, soothing voice spoke from her side.

"It's okay, Christina. You hit your head but we're doing some tests. I need you to lay still for me. Can you do that?" the voice asked.

Christina? Who is Christina?

"Jill," she heard herself croak. Her voice didn't seem to be working.

"Shh. Try not to talk, dear. Is Jill your friend? She's waiting for you in your room. We'll get you back there in no time. You just relax for one more minute for me." The voice was so soothing.

Jill heard someone ask for a neuro consult. That was the last thing she heard before she drifted off again.

∽

Jill opened her eyes and tried to take in the room around her. Small. Beige walls. IV in her arm. Hospital. And someone was speaking to her.

"Wakey, wakey, Jill. Time to go for a ride."

She felt a bite of pain in her forearm and looked down to see her IV had been ripped out. She turned her head toward the voice and saw a woman who looked vaguely familiar. Where had she seen her before?

The woman put her arms under Jill and dragged her off the bed. Her body felt like rubber. She couldn't move her arms or legs as she was dumped into a wheelchair.

Panic began to settle in her belly as confusion washed over her. Something wasn't right. The woman pushed and pulled until Jill was sitting, albeit slumped over, in the wheelchair.

She felt the chair begin to move and as the chair crossed the threshold of the room, a foggy part of Jill's brain was screaming out to her to stay. Stay in the room where she was safe.

Elevator doors. Sliding open and then closed.

Jill's chair was pushed next to the buttons by the door and the woman spoke again.

"Hmmm. Up or down? Up or down?" The woman spoke in a sing-songy voice. "I wonder if there's a furnace in the basement? That's probably only in the movies, huh? Roof it is then, little whore. You can jump from the roof. Poor Andrew will have to do the obligatory mourning thing for a while, but don't worry, I'll be there to see him through it."

Jill's head was beginning to clear and her limbs were coming back to life. The rubbery feeling was slipping away, but she kept her head down, stayed slumped over as she processed.

This was the woman who hit Jill with her car. Hit her with a rock. And stability didn't seem to be in this woman's repertoire. But what was her connection to Andrew? What was going on?

Jill knew she needed to stop this before they reached the rooftop. Keeping her body still, she thought things through. The elevator wouldn't go all the way to the roof. They'd have to get off at the top floor and then use the stairs.

Would the top floor have people on it? Should she wait until they were off the elevator and then call for help?

Jill was facing the wall of the elevator. The woman stood behind the wheelchair. Could she shove the chair back and fight?

No. Better to wait until there were other people around to help her. Because the way she felt, she didn't have a whole lot of fight in her.

～

As they climbed into Jason's Suburban, Andrew asked Kelly for the list of hospitals she had called. Kelly handed him her iPhone with the search results for nearby hospitals on the screen.

"You asked about Jane Does and Jill Walsh?" Andrew asked as he scanned the list. Four hospitals. Two to the north and two to the south.

"Yes. None of them had anyone like that," Kelly said.

Andrew punched the number for the first hospital into his phone and then tossed Kelly's phone back to her. "Call the second one and ask for any unusual IDs," he said and then began to speak into his phone when someone picked up at the hospital.

"Hello. We're looking for a missing woman. I understand you have no Jane Does there, but can you tell me if anyone was brought into the emergency room with any unusual form of ID? Someone else providing the ID or an ID that maybe didn't look like the person? An ID that doesn't look real?"

Kelly gave out phone numbers for the others to call. Andrew heard the woman on the other end of his phone talk to other voices in the background before coming back with an answer for him. They'd had nothing like that.

Andrew hung up just as Jack and Jennie were hanging up their phones. They both shook their heads at Andrew. Chad was still on hold.

"Which way now?" Jason asked Andrew as they approached the highway.

Andrew had no idea what the hell he was doing. It seemed ludicrous to think if Theresa took her, Jill would have somehow made it to a hospital. But even so, for some reason, Andrew's gut was telling him Jill was in one of those hospitals. He could feel it in his bones.

He just prayed he was right. Because if Jill really was up on that mountain and he was taking them further away from her, he would never forgive himself.

"South. The only other hospital is south. Head there," Andrew said, saying a silent prayer over and over.

Chad hung up the phone. "I'm getting the runaround at the last hospital. It's one thing for them to say they have no Jane Doe's but they won't say if they have anyone who might be Jill under a different name. Jason, maybe you can make it an official inquiry?"

Jason continued speeding down the highway, eating up the road between them and the last hospital. He grabbed his radio and spoke into the mic. "Dispatch, I need you to patch me through to Angels of Mercy Hospital."

The radio crackled and the gravelly, female voice of a long-time smoker came through. "I was just about to radio you. I've got an Officer Kelter on the line. Thinks he saw your missing woman earlier. You want me to patch him through or get you the hospital?"

"Patch," Jason answered quickly.

It took a minute before another voice came on the line.

"Jason? It's Matt Kelter. I think I saw your missing woman a couple of hours ago. Pulled over a woman for speeding. She said her friend had been in an accident and she was trying to get her help. The friend was there clear as day in the backseat with a gash in her head, so I gave an escort. The friend didn't try to run off when we got there or anything. Sat in the waiting room to wait for news. They're at Mercy now. Well, at least they were when I left."

Andrew felt both a wave of relief and a wave of anguish wash over him. Theresa must have gotten caught speeding and done the only thing she could. Made up some bullshit story to cover the fact that Jill had been knocked out and lying in her backseat.

But Andrew had no idea what Theresa would do now. Would she run, leaving Jill safely at the hospital? Or would she remain, trying to get Jill out of there or get into her room to hurt her? Never mind his worry over the head wound Jill had. No telling what Theresa did to Jill before that cop found them.

Jason's foot pressed on the gas, increasing his speed and Andrew was grateful for the red flashing lights of the Fire Chief's truck.

"Kelter, I need you to call Mercy. We're four minutes away but the woman Jill is with is dangerous. They need to take her into custody and get her away from Jill," Jason barked into the phone.

"Got it," the officer said and the connection was broken.

Jason exited the highway and turned right, following the large blue H signs to the hospital. As they pulled into the lot, the radio crackled to life.

"Jason, the room is empty and both women are missing. They're searching the hospital now and they have it on lockdown," Matt's voice reported.

"Shit," Andrew said as he ran for the hospital doors. A guard was shaking his head 'no' at Andrew through the locked glass doors, but Jason and the others caught up to him and Jason's credentials got them through the door.

CHAPTER 46

Jill kept her head down but listened carefully to the *ping* of the elevator as it traveled up the floors.

Why isn't anyone else getting on the elevator? This is crazy.

Out of the corner of her eye, she saw Theresa move. She was holding something, but Jill couldn't see what it was.

"Time for a little cocktail party for you, Jill. I think this is a sedative. I hope so anyway. Snagged it from one of the nurses. Time to knock your ass out so you can't cause any trouble while I figure out how to get you on the roof."

Now or never. Please let this work.

Jill hit the alarm button on the elevator panel and shoved the wheelchair back as hard as she could, using her legs to push off the wall in front of her. It wasn't a direct hit, but her captor went flying against the elevator wall just the same.

Jill stood and turned, but her legs were weak. She mostly stumbled into the woman, wrapped her arms around her waist and pushed her into the wall again. Jill managed to raise her arm and grab the kidnapper's hair and slam her head into the elevator wall before Jill fell, her strength depleted.

As Andrew listened to hospital security explain that they were searching the floors of the hospital – all ten floors with a staff of six security officers – he knew they needed a better plan. It would take forever to find Jill and who knew what Theresa might do to her in that time.

He slipped from the room. Screw waiting around like they'd been instructed. Jack and Chad exited the room with him. Jason gave him a look and continued to chat up the head of hospital security, hopefully distracting him long enough for Andrew, Chad, and Jack to find Jill on their own. Kelly and Jennie were waiting out in the hall and approached as soon as the three men left the room.

"All right, Andrew. Your gut has worked for us on this so far. Turn on your Jill homing signal and tell us where to look," said Chad.

"Sorry, I don't have shit. I have no idea where to look now." Andrew had never felt so hopeless as he eyed the clock on the wall wondering how much time Jill had left.

"Let's think like a crazy chick," Jennie said. Everyone turned expectantly and her face clouded. "What, me? Why do I have to pretend to have the crazies?" She received pointed looks in answer and waved a hand. "Okay, okay. Good point."

Jennie shook out her arms and legs as if getting into character and stared at the ceiling. Then at the floor... Then the ceiling... Then the floor.

"Roof or basement. That's where I'd go. Roof or basement." Jennie nodded her head at the group.

"Good," Andrew said. "Chad, take the basement. Jack and I will hit the roof. Jennie and Kelly can you stay here and call us if these guys find anything?" Andrew jerked his head toward the security office.

The three men took off running. Just as they arrived at the

bank of elevators, the alarm went off in one of them. All three men shared a silent look that spoke volumes. They homed in on the elevator that was making all the noise and checked the lighted number above it.

"Fourth floor. Jack, call me if it starts moving again," Andrew said and he and Chad ran for the stairwell. Even in the stairwell, the men could hear the tinny ring of the elevator alarm. When they hit the third floor the alarm stopped.

Andrew's phone rang seconds later.

"Talk to me, Jack. Which way?" Andrew asked.

"Up," came Jack's voice through the phone. "They're going up."

Chad and Andrew continued to run the flights.

"Let me know if it stops," Andrew said into the phone and then pressed his body into high gear. Chad was ahead of him, taking the steps in triple time without breaking a sweat. Andrew's legs burned, but not as much as the pain in his heart at the thought they might not make it in time.

Up and up and up. Andrew pictured Jill waiting for him. Praying for him to get there. He just hoped she could hang on long enough. Panting, he lifted the phone to his ear and spoke.

"Anything, Jack?"

"No. They're still going up. They're on nine now but still going up. Get to the tenth floor."

The last floor marker they had passed had said eighth floor. They were two behind.

"On tenth, Chad. They're almost there," Andrew said, picking up his pace, putting everything he had into it. Chad did the same.

Chad and Andrew burst through the door to the tenth-floor moments later, but the floor was quiet. Eerily silent. It was a floor filled with offices that appeared to be empty for the weekend. The men stood and listened.

A shrill scream.

"Rooftop," Chad said, pointing to another door at the end of the hall marked Rooftop Access.

∼

Jill was barely hanging on by a thread. There were black spots at the periphery of her vision and her body felt sluggish. Slow to respond. She'd been unable to fight as her attacker dragged her from the elevator and up the stairwell.

She felt battered and bruised by the repetitive knocking of the stairs. Her mind grasped at threads of ideas, wisps of defenses, any way to ward off the blows and escape what was clearly a completely insane woman.

The woman dragged Jill out onto the roof of the building and let Jill's body drop to the rooftop. The woman was winded and clearly agitated. She circled Jill, ranting about Jill's manipulations, her scheming against Andrew.

Jill went back into possum mode and lay huddled on the ground, regaining her strength. Planning. Preparing.

She focused on her breathing, steadying it. She cracked her eyelids open to see where her kidnapper was and she watched, waiting for the woman to come close. Jill could hear the woman trying to catch her breath – as if she, too, were readying for something.

She didn't want to know what that something was. She had a pretty good idea that it had to do with the edge of the roof and Jill going over it.

"Well," the woman said, taking a deep breath, "it's that time. Any last words before you go?" She laughed the laugh of a crazy loon as if she had made the joke of the century.

"You know, I wasn't going to do this. I was going to let you confess all you'd done and record it so Andrew could finally learn the truth about you. But I can't do that now that we're here."

She looked around. "I'll tell them I followed you up here

because I was worried about your state of mind. That I thought maybe you'd run your car off the road on purpose. That I tried to stop you from jumping but couldn't."

Jill watched through slitted eyes as the woman came toward her and bent over, placing her hands under Jill's arms to prepare to lift her again.

Without hesitation, Jill struck. Thumbs gouged as hard as she could into the woman's eyes. The scream of pain was all Jill heard as she got to her knees and crawled toward the door to the building. She felt one hand clutch at her ankle but she kicked out as hard as she could and then kept moving.

Move. Just keep moving, keep trying. Don't stop.

One minute she was crawling and the next she was hallucinating. Jill's emotions were ripped to shreds as she realized if hallucinations had taken over, she was probably done for.

She had no more fight left in her. She let her weight sink into her illusion that Andrew's arms were really around her. That she could really hear Andrew whispering words of safety and love to her as she lay wrecked in his arms.

CHAPTER 47

Andrew's whole body shuddered with relief when he finally had Jill in his arms. She had fought. He'd seen her.

She'd gotten away long enough for Chad and Andrew to get to her. As Chad subdued a shrieking Theresa, Jill sank into Andrew's arms and he dropped to the rooftop and held her tight.

He rocked Jill and whispered to her. "I've got you, sweetheart. You're safe now." Over and over he whispered the words. "I won't let you go."

And he didn't. Not while they treated her wounds. Not while they began an IV to rehydrate her. Not while she finally slept. Andrew held her all through the night, laying kisses on her temple whenever she began to dream or toss in her sleep.

When Jill woke in the morning, she blinked up at him, confusion washing over her features.

"I thought you were a hallucination. I thought I imagined you. That you were a dream," she whispered.

"The only dream here is you, Jill. You're my dream, my heart, my future. I thought I'd lost you forever. Don't ever leave me, Jill."

EPILOGUE

Andrew didn't let Jill out of his sight for a week. Kelly took Jill to the support group she'd found after her ordeal—a group for survivors of violent crime. Jill hadn't wanted to go, but she had to admit, it felt good to meet people who had been through similar situations. Everyone's story was different, but they shared similar emotions and struggled with similar obstacles as they tried to settle back into everyday life.

Theresa was arrested, but she was currently residing in a state mental health facility where she was receiving treatment for a host of issues. Jill knew it was a little odd, but she couldn't help feeling badly for Theresa on some level. The woman was struggling with several mental illnesses.

She had apparently received treatment for them when she was younger, but had lost her insurance several years before. When she got on the Sutton Capital Insurance Policy, she never sought the help she needed. Most likely, by that point, she no longer recognized her need for help.

Jill felt Andrew's strong arms come around her waist. She hugged his arms closer to her, reveling in the feeling of safety and security she felt when she was with him. Not only security from people like Theresa, but security for her future. She believed, with all her heart, that her love for Andrew would never die. And, she knew his love for her was strong enough to last two lifetimes. They would never part the way she and Jake had.

Jill smiled whenever she thought of the young Andrew Weston that watched her so many summers ago. Perhaps it was fate or kismet that neither had found lasting love with anyone else. Perhaps they always belonged to each other.

"How are you feeling, sweetheart?" Andrew asked, dipping his head to the nape of her neck to bury his face in her hair.

She was used to hearing this question quite frequently now, but she knew he meant well. He didn't mean to be overbearing. She turned in his arms and wrapped her arms around his neck.

"I'm perfect, now. Just perfect," she said as she stood on tiptoes and raised her lips to his. Andrew's response was instant and she felt the familiar thrill at being able to arouse him so quickly and thoroughly.

He scooped her up, causing a shriek and a laugh to fall from her lips.

"I bet I can make you even better," he said as he strode toward the stairs with Jill in his arms.

"You'd mess with perfection?" Jill laughed.

He growled and claimed her lips as he brought Jill down on the bed. And within minutes, she was very, very glad that Andrew had been bold enough to mess with perfection.

Three months later ...

Andrew hadn't wanted to leave the house. Not once he'd seen Jill in the deep red dress she was wearing. There was probably a name for it. Burgundy or ruby or something. He couldn't care less what the name was.

He'd wanted to fall to his knees when he saw her and then convince her they should stay home instead.

He would have made a convincing argument, too, were it not for the fact Jack and Kelly had picked them up. They had agreed to drive together to the fund raiser.

Now, Jack and Andrew stood off to one side of the room. It was a fundraising event for a charity he'd gladly write a check for so they could leave, but the women said they needed to spend at least an hour making the rounds first.

"Waiting for something or just checking the time?" Andrew asked when Jack checked his phone for the tenth time. It was possible his friend was just as eager to bail as he was.

It was a miracle they'd gotten a quiet few minutes to themselves without people wanting to talk to them.

"No, checking to see if Zach called. He said he'd call when he finished with a job."

Andrew raised a brow. Zach was the bodyguard who helped Kelly out after she was kidnapped. He ran a private security firm and had done a lot of work for Jack in the past.

"Everything all right?"

Jack rubbed a hand on the back of his neck, a trademark Jack Sutton stress signal. Andrew hadn't seen it nearly as much lately, but it was clear Jack was tense about something.

"No. Kelly's mom came to see me today. Jesse is having trouble." Jesse was Kelly's sister.

"What kind of trouble? Is someone threatening her?" Andrew saw Jill and Kelly working their way toward them from across the room.

"I haven't told Kelly about it yet," Jack said, turning his body slightly so he faced more toward Andrew and less toward the two women approaching them. "I'll fill you in later. She's safe, but she's going to need Zach's help."

Andrew frowned but then felt Jill's hand on his arm. She leaned toward him, smiling as she raised a hand and brushed at the furrow between his brows.

"The fundraiser's not that bad," Jill said, laughter lacing her words. She grinned at Kelly. "I guess we've hit our hour mark."

Andrew put his arm around Jill's waist and pulled her to him. He wanted to get her home. Wanted to take her to bed.

He looked to Jack. "Fill me in tomorrow?"

Jack nodded and Andrew kissed Kelly on the cheek and watched as she and Jill hugged goodbye.

And then he had her moving toward the exit.

There wasn't an ounce of annoyance in Jill's eyes or tone when she chastised him. "You realize it took me an hour and a half to get ready for this thing. This makeup and hair didn't do itself."

He leaned in, putting his mouth close to her ear. "And I appreciate every last bit of it. Those smoky eyes are going to look gorgeous beneath me when I make you scream my name."

She turned and batted at him with her hand, but she was laughing.

Still, when he got her out to the car and got her settled into the passenger seat, he saw passion burning in her eyes for him. She was just as eager to get home as he was. She murmured something about his tux before pulling him toward her for a kiss.

There was nothing about life with Jill he didn't love. Nothing at all. And it was time he took her home and proved it to her.

Showing her how much he loved her would never get old. It wasn't something he'd ever tire of.

He knew life wouldn't be perfect. Love was something you worked at. Had to work at if you wanted to keep it. But it was a job he was willing to take on. It was a life he was willing to fight for, for the rest of his life.

The End

Thank you so much for reading! Wasn't Andrew Weston positively dreamy? I crushed on him hard! But, listen, Jesse and Chad deserve their story, don't they? They've waited for it a long time. It's not an easy one. They have a lot to go through together.

Suspense, heartache, steamy, sexy oh-so-hot times. You know, all the good stuff! Grab The Billionaire Op here and binge now! loriryanromance.com/book/the-billionaire-op

Read on for chapter one of The Billionaire Op:

CHAPTER ONE

Chad Thompson woke to searing pain in his chest as he gulped air, desperate to fill his battered lungs. He squeezed his eyes shut and battled to clear the fog from his head and slow his heart rate.

This was wrong. It was all wrong. He caught hold of the sounds around him and forced himself to listen to them, knowing they would ground him: the sound of traffic on the street below his window and the hum of his air conditioner kicking on as it reached the designated temperature. Chad shook his head and forced his eyes open.

He was in his bedroom in New Haven, Connecticut, in his bed with the navy-blue sheets and mahogany headboard. Above him was the familiar crack on the ceiling that he always meant to fix but never remembered to unless he was in bed staring up at it. His flat-screen television, mounted on the wall, ran static. His laptop lay on the bed next to him where he'd abandoned it for sleep the night before.

Despite the familiar surroundings, it took Chad a minute to realize there was no medic kneeling beside him, pushing a too-long needle into his lung. There was no metallic scent of blood or charred flesh choking him and making him nauseated.

No ringing in his ears. The other three men in his detail did not lay still and silent beside him, their eyes lifeless and unseeing, their bodies forever broken and destroyed.

The dream didn't come often anymore, but it always took him a few minutes to recover when it did. As Chad took deep, calming breaths he realized his phone was ringing. He slapped at the nightstand with one hand until he found the phone then slid his thumb across the screen to answer the call.

"Yeah?" His voice was thick with sleep.

"Chad?"

He bolted upright in his bed, the remnants of the dream no longer clutching at him. His gut twisted when Jennie's voice came through the phone with the ring of false confidence. Something wasn't right.

"You okay, Jennie?"

Jennie Evans didn't normally call him outside of working hours at Sutton Capital. They had a weird relationship. Chad was Jennie's boss. She was flippant, irreverent, and completely brash in all her dealings with him. And, he loved it.

Outside of work, things were equally unorthodox between them. They spent a lot of time together because Jennie was best friends with Kelly, the woman who married Chad's cousin last year. Jack and Chad were more like brothers than cousins. So Chad saw Jennie almost anytime he hung out with Jack and Kelly, which was just about every weekend.

But, Chad and Jennie weren't the type of friends that called each other or sought one another out outside of the group. It was more that they ended up at the same functions because of their mutual relationships.

So when she called on his cell phone first thing on a Sunday morning, he noticed.

It was also the use of his name that got his attention. Quickly.

Jennie didn't use a nickname like 'Boss Man,' 'Big Man,' or 'the Hulk' like she usually did. No, this morning she called him Chad, rather than any number of other nicknames designed to taunt him about his large stature.

"Um. I'm a little...stuck," Jennie said on the other end of the phone. He could hear her hesitancy through the line.

"Define 'stuck,' Jennie." As he talked, he threw back the covers and swung his legs over the edge of the bed.

"I'm out at Edgerton Park and I don't have any shoes to jog home. Can you come get me? Jack and Kelly are touring the Labor and Delivery Unit at the hospital this morning so I can't call them and I can't get hold of Jill, either" Jennie said.

Jill was married to Chad's friend Andrew who also worked at Sutton Capital.

"How did you get out to Edgerton Park without shoes or a car?" Chad asked as he shoved his feet into sneakers.

As he spoke, the implications of what he'd just said sank into his brain. Jennie was alone in a park without shoes or a way to get home. Fear for her rippled up his spine, but he tamped it down and focused.

He moved a lot faster, as his mind began to play through scenarios. Was she with a guy and he ditched her? Was she out drunk last night and never made it home? Maybe she found herself in the park, with no shoes and no idea how she got there?

Just the thought of Jennie out with a guy started a slow burn in his gut, not that he had any right to be upset about that. Chad couldn't date her since he was her boss, but if a man treated her wrong or hurt her in any way. . . he sure as hell wouldn't tolerate that.

I'll kill whatever asshole did this to her.

"Can I tell you when you get here? I've been here for a while now. I'm getting a little hungry. And my feet hurt. I had to run in bare feet. I could really use a ride."

Run? She'd been running...

Chad's fists turned into hard knots of anger as he thought about someone leaving Jennie where she could have been hurt or... Another thought sent cold spiraling through him.

God, what if they didn't just ditch her at the park? What if...? His heart pounded in his chest and he broke out in a sweat.

Now Chad used the eerily calm tone of voice from his days in the military. It came out when he was pissed as hell and ready to tear someone to pieces, but also when he needed to keep himself calm and collected enough to deal with the situation.

"Jennie, did someone hurt you?"

"I'm okay, Chad. No one hurt me," she answered, sending a wave of relief over him that left him weak—much weaker than he'd acknowledge. He grabbed his wallet and keys.

"On my way."

"Thanks, Chad. I'm over by the greenhouses. I'll wait by that entrance," Jennie said.

The park was well known for the large row of greenhouses that boasted an impressive array of native plants. The local gardening club held a native plant sale twice a year. There was an entrance cut into the stone wall that surrounded the park, near those greenhouses. Chad knew it well. It was the entrance he used whenever he jogged through the park.

"Got it," Chad said as he ended the call and grabbed a T-shirt. He pulled the shirt on as he rode the elevator to the garage and jogged to his truck.

What the hell, Jennie?

He didn't know what story she'd have when he got there, but this sounded like a bit much, even for Jennie.

Explaining this to Chad wouldn't be fun. How do you explain that you had to run from guard dogs with half your clothes missing because they snuck up on you when you were skinny dipping in some guy's pool?

When Jennie had been running from the dogs, she was laughing. When she'd climbed the fence and run through a stranger's backyard to get away, it had still been kind of funny. When she couldn't find anyone other than Chad to come out and get her, she'd stopped laughing.

Kelly or Jill would have laughed with her. Even Jack or

Andrew probably would have laughed a little. Chad? Not so much. He wouldn't be amused and he wouldn't hesitate to lecture her. And lecture her. And lecture her.

She spotted Chad's black F350 as he turned onto Cliff Street. She had to force herself to stand still and keep her head raised. If she fidgeted, he'd see it as a sign of weakness and that would only make things worse.

Jennie twisted her long hair, squeezing the excess water from it. What a sight she must be. Her hair was wet, she was missing her shoes and her bra, and her T-shirt was torn and dirty. And if he noticed her limping, he'd probably drag her off to the hospital. Chad was nothing, if not overprotective.

And...there's the scowl.

Jennie wished, for once, he wouldn't look so damned sexy. She didn't know how it was possible for someone to look so good and still have such an angry expression, but he looked gorgeous no matter what he was doing.

Maybe it was the dangerous edge he presented. Anyone who knew Chad knew he was a sweet teddy bear on the inside, but on the outside he looked like he could do some serious damage.

On a sigh, Jennie opened the door and climbed up into the large cab of Chad's truck. She knew he'd picked his truck to fit himself comfortably. Unfortunately, it dwarfed everyone else, making it a project for Jennie to get in and out. She shimmied up and plopped into the passenger seat.

Settling herself, Jennie buckled her seatbelt and raised her face to Chad's. She tilted her head to the side and took in Chad's brooding gaze. A shiver of awareness went through her body as she felt his damn eyes on her.

Down, girl.

As usual, her body refused to listen to her when it came to Chad. It ran amuck, responding to every look, every whisper, and every grumble that came from those sexy lips in that low, controlled tone of his. Oh, what she wouldn't do to see him lose that control.

No! I don't want that. It's only my stupid, traitorous body that wants that.

"Hey, Tiny," she said. "I'd offer to buy you breakfast, but with no shoes, I'm afraid we couldn't get in anywhere respectable."

She put on her best cheeky grin and hoped he would ignore the embarrassing state of her clothing. Or, lack thereof.

Chad was apparently of a different mind and let his eyes roam from her face, down her body and back up again. Of course, his gaze felt like hands grazing her body and that lit her up from the inside. Somehow, she knew his hands would feel even more amazing on her. Caressing, roaming freely, they would set her ablaze.

Stupid body.

He kept his eyes on hers as he reached over and turned off the ignition with a short, economic movement. Then, he sat. Waited.

Great. He's in interrogation mode.

She rolled her eyes. "Really?"

"Really." His was a statement not a question and she realized that, yes, he really was going to wait until she spilled the story. She sighed heavily, hoping he would give up.

Damn. The man's got military training and I've got diddly.

"You realize I'm an adult, right? I don't actually need to tell you what I was doing. You get that, right?"

Jennie could have sworn she saw the side of his mouth twitch and wondered for a split second if he was tempted to smile. *No. Not Chad.*

"I can always let you out and just go home, Jennie. I'm an adult. I don't actually need to drive you home. You get that, right?" he mimicked her words.

She narrowed her eyes at him. "You wouldn't..."

Chad shrugged as if he really might consider leaving Jennie there. They both knew he wouldn't.

"I was jogging. All right? I jog out here every morning." She laid her hands in her lap as if that answered everything and looked back at Chad with what she hoped was her best wide-eyed and innocent gaze. Oh, why did her belly feel like a hundred can-can girls were practicing in there with their puffy can-can skirts whipping around?

One tanned, muscled arm rested on the steering wheel of the truck, the other lay between him and Jennie on the seat. She tried not to notice the muscles rippling under his T-shirt or how good he smelled.

He'd clearly been sleeping when she called him. He probably just rolled out of bed, threw on sweats – and he somehow managed to look like walking sex and smell spicy and woodsy... She licked her lips.

Chad, who'd been studying her face, looked pointedly down at her bare feet, then flicked his eyes back up to hers and waited. That earned him another eye roll and a huff of frustration.

"Fine. I jog out here every morning. There's a house on Prospect Court that has a pool. The guy is never home. He travels a lot," Jennie explained in clipped tones.

"You know this, how?" Chad asked, but made no move to start the truck.

She could see the small tick in his jaw that struck when she was really needling him. Sometimes, she could turn the tick into a smile, if she worked hard at it. She wondered if she'd be able to do that now, but wasn't sure she could risk it. If she pushed too hard at the wrong time, things might go in the other direction and she'd be in for a lecture.

Not that a lecture from him was all that bad. She could zone out and stare at the way his shirt stretched across the hard planes of his chest or the evidence of a six pack she could see just below it. But, she would like to shower sooner rather than later. She was starting to feel really grimy.

"My friend dated him for a while," Jennie shrugged. "Can we go now?"

Chad raised an eyebrow but remained silent.

A frustrated sigh burst past Jennie's lips, as she shook her head at him. "Fine, I jog here, let myself in through the back gate, go for a swim, and then jog home. It's my morning routine. I always peek to see if his car's in the garage. If it is, I skip my swim. He must have realized someone's been in his yard. I had just gotten in the pool when I heard barking. The next thing I know, there are two big dogs blasting out of a doggy door and heading my way. They were on the side of the yard with the gate, so I had to go over the back of the fence instead and cut through the neighbor's yard. I grabbed what I could and ran. My shoes weren't in the pile of stuff I grabbed."

Jennie drew her spine up straight and laced her fingers together in her lap. It wasn't easy to look dignified in the state she was in, but she could damn well try.

Chad stared at Jennie for a few more long seconds. The tick in his jaw continued as his eyes burned into her with an intensity that almost stole her breath. She raised her chin and resisted the very strong urge to squirm.

"Neither was your bra, apparently," he said dryly as he reached for the keys and started the truck. He shoved the gear into place and pulled away from the curb as Jennie laughed, wrapping her arms firmly in place over her chest.

Get The Billionaire Op here! loriryanromance.com/book/the-billionaire-op

ABOUT THE AUTHOR

Lori Ryan is a NY Times and USA Today bestselling author who writes contemporary romance and romantic suspense. She lives with an extremely understanding husband, three wonderful children, and two dogs (who are lucky they're adorable and cute because they rarely behave) in Austin, Texas. It's a bit of a zoo, but she wouldn't change a thing.

Lori published her first novel in April of 2013 and has loved every bit of the crazy adventure this career has taken her on since then. Lori loves to connect with her readers. Follow her on Facebook or Twitter or subscribe to her blog. Oh, and if you've read Lori's books and loved them, please consider leaving a review with the retailer of your choice to help other readers find her work as well! It's a tremendous honor to have her work recommended to others or written up in reviews. Lori promises to do a happy dance around her office every time you write one!

facebook.com/loriryanromance
twitter.com/Loriryanauthor
instagram.com/loriryanauthor

.

Made in the USA
Columbia, SC
22 April 2021